D1742089

THE DARKNESS WITHIN

J.W. Holmes

I would like to thank my mum, and all of my family and friends for supporting me in writing this story.

I

In the early hours of the morning, he watched the crescent moon weave back and forth between the clouds above. The constant rumbling of the engine drowned out all other sounds. The ocean was silent. He felt the waves crash against the hull of his boat, but heard nothing. The water flew over the sides and dampened his boots. The clouds seemed to disappear entirely, and the moon had now become a permanent fixture in the black sky.

He pulled slowly back on the acceleration, bringing his boat to a dead stop. He could now hear everything around him. The rhythmic droning of the waves moving around him, and the midnight breeze whispering across the ocean like a skipping stone. A large black duffle bag sat beside him on the floor. He knelt down beside it and opened it. Her utterly still and motionless face leapt out as if she was desperate for a breath of air, but she was dead, her eyes void of all life. Her mouth was wide open and her teeth were blackened. Caked in blood. He opened the bag fully revealing her broken and contorted body. She was shaped like a pretzel the way she was squeezed into the bag. She was completely covered in a thin film of blood. It had congealed, and she had become formless under it.

He reached under her and lifted her out of the bag. Her joints cracked as her limbs stretched out and became whole again. The blood stuck to his skin, and he cringed at the sensation. He looked at her one last time, then he looked around to make sure they were alone. Water splashed high over the railing as her body landed in the ocean. He watched her as she sank slowly into the depths and he felt nothing.

◆ ◆ ◆

It was nearing dawn and Greene sat in the chair by her bed looking out of the slim gap between the curtains at the moon sitting idly in the sky. She couldn't sleep, just as she couldn't the night before and many nights before that. When she tried to sleep the most horrible of dreams visited her, so she avoided sleeping altogether, preferring the companionship of the headaches and nausea garnered from her self-inflicted insomnia. It was a warm summer night, and she wore nothing but her plain black briefs. The sound of her phone ringing startled her. She sat up straight in her chair, reached over and switched on the lamp on the bedside table. The light was bright and blinded her for a moment. She picked up her phone, which lay next to her badge and her holstered gun. She disconnected the charger and answered.

"Yeah?" she said.

"Hey, it's Paul. Sorry for calling so early. I just assumed you'd be awake."

"I'm awake. What time is it? Is something wrong?"

"Oh, no. I just wanted to check that we're still on for mass this morning?"

She rubbed her weary eyes. "I'll be there," she said.

"Great! Alex will be pleased to see you. We'll see you soon then?"

"Yeah, I'll see you soon."

She ended the call, tossed her phone onto the bed, and relaxed back into her chair. She was half asleep, and she rubbed her eyes again. She stood and walked over to her ensuite bathroom. She took a brief cold shower to wake herself up and completed all her usual necessities. Her hair smelled of milk and honey afterwards. She finished washing her face and splashed it with water from the sink then looked at herself in the mirror. She ran her fingers across the bottom of her eyelids and then down her cheeks. She looked tired. She dried her face with her towel, then opened up the cabinet and took out a pill bottle. Diazepam. She threw two in her mouth and swallowed them dry.

She then went to her bedroom wardrobe and picked out her suit. It was a simple two-piece suit consisting of a white button-down shirt with a matching grey jacket and pants. It was the only suit she owned and she used it for both work and formal occasions. She wasn't completely sure which this was. She placed it on the bed and closed her wardrobe. She grabbed her bra off of her dresser and put it on then put on her suit. Finally, she tied her long blonde hair into a loose ponytail and looked at herself in the mirror. It'll do, she thought.

In the kitchen she poured herself a cup of lukewarm day-old coffee and drank it quickly, suffering the bitter taste. She stood, leaning on her faux marble countertop. She watched the clock on the wall tick forward. Half mesmerized by it, she waited. Before she left, she grabbed her phone, badge, and gun, and put them all on her person then she checked herself in the mirror once more. As she left her apartment her neighbour Mrs. Driscoll was leaving hers. Mrs. Driscoll had turned seventy years old just a week earlier but you wouldn't have been able to tell. She was a kind and exceedingly polite woman whom Greene always considered to be the best neighbour imaginable. Quiet and solitude.

"Oh!" Mrs. Driscoll said, clutching her chest in surprise. "Good morning, dear!"

"Good morning, Mrs. Driscoll," Greene said.

They both locked their respective doors and walked down the hall together.

"Are you going to morning mass as well?" Mrs. Driscoll asked.

"I am! Can I give you a lift?"

"Oh no, thank you! My son is taking me, he's waiting outside."

"How nice of him."

"Yes, he's a sweet boy. He and his wife, Kate, just moved five minutes away so they're always driving me here and there."

"That's very nice!"

"Oh yes, it's a blessing for certain."

They walked down the stairs of their building to the street and they saw the sun beginning to reveal itself beyond the horizon. Mrs. Driscoll's son was waiting by his car and she walked over to him and they both waved at Greene, and then they left.

Greene drove a grey 2015 Toyota Corolla that she kept parked outside in her designated space. When she got in she took her badge and gun and put them in the glovebox. It was 7:45am when Greene drove out to the church. The drive was uneventful and swift. There was no traffic this early in the morning, although there wouldn't be much on a Sunday regardless of the time. It was pleasant to see the small New England town of Piscator Bay in this light. The town was shrouded in shadow except for the few houses that sat on the hills to the west that were lit up by the dawning sun. The town was empty, it looked and felt like a ghost town. A memory of a bygone era. She had to drive through the town centre to get to the church. She drove past her precinct then she passed by the post office, The Colossal Squid Inn, King's Bookstore, and the sole grocery store in town. All remained in a state of limbo.

She passed the town square which was inhabited solely by flocks of birds. Gulls and pigeons. At the centre of the square was a tall bronze statue of a Union soldier standing dutifully in his uniform with his rifle by his side to commemorate the men who fought and died in the Civil War. She kept driving through the old cobbled streets until the church spire was visible in all of its majesty. She turned into a large parking lot outside of the hundred-foot tall church which sat on the corner of a quiet suburban street. The church was one of two in the town. This one was the largest - it could entertain a thousand people - and the oldest. Built in 1812, it was also the oldest building still standing in town. As she got out of the car, a woman she didn't know was getting out of the car next to hers. They greeted each other. They walked together through a thin iron archway and down the stone path to the church entrance. Inside, a man waved at her from the third pew as she entered through the vestibule. He was a short man, with kind eyes and handsome features. He wore a v-neck sweater and was holding hands with a young girl, who was barely of school age. She waved back at him then walked down the aisle, and shuffled down the pew to sit beside him.

The little girl moved across the pew so that she sat between them. She wrapped her arms around Greene's waist. Greene put her hand gently on the girl's head and stroked her hair.

"Hi Alex, sweetie," Greene said.

"I'm glad you came, we both are," the man said, leaning over.

She looked up from the girl, "Me too, Paul," she said, smiling.

The monolithic church slowly filled with people keen to hear the reverend's word. Families of all sizes, dragging their bored children in tow. To the elderly, widows and widowers coming to search for some semblance of peace. After everyone had sat down, the reverend appeared from the doorway beyond the altar and walked up to the pulpit. The sunlight shone through the windows in front of him and brightened his experienced visage. The choir stood behind him in two rows. The whispers between the churchgoers subsided and the room became silent. He straightened his frock and laid a bible on the top of the lectern and opened it to the intended page.

"Good morning," said the reverend. "Thank you all for coming. Before we begin the hymns I would like to talk to you today about justice. About fairness. I have my bible turned to Leviticus 19:15, which says: 'Ye shall do no unrighteousness in judgement. Thou shalt not respect the person of the poor, nor honor the person of the mighty, but in righteousness shalt thou judge thy neighbour.' What does this mean? What is God trying to tell us? Well, I for one believe that this verse is asking us to be fair in our judgements of others, regardless of who they may be. If you are wronged, you may get angry, even become vengeful. I'm sure we've all had our own experiences.

"But we must, as a people, as a community, not succumb to that temptation. You see it every day on the news, people and governments using vengeance as an excuse, a justification, to commit great atrocities. Often times in the name of God. God doesn't wish that. No! God asks us to be forgiving and even when forgiveness is an impossibility we must still be fair and just. Because isn't that what we're all taught - To love thy neighbor? Does He mean one neighbor over the other? No! He means all of our neighbors regardless of who they are, or what they believe. That's what love is. Acceptance of others. Who are we to choose when that love is no longer welcome?"

The audience listened intently to the reverend and nodded in approval at the end of each sentence.

"I'm reminded of a story, a parable you could call it," the reverend continued. "My father told me this when I was a young boy and he was the priest here, some of you may remember him. This was a long time ago. A man in a village was beset by grief when a drunken driver crashed into his daughter while she was riding her bike home from a friend's place. She died. And the driver was punished. He was sentenced to prison. I think we can all agree that this was a just punishment. I'm sure the driver did not mean to kill the girl but his careless and selfish actions led to her death. So he had to be punished. However, the father did not believe the punishment was enough. He planned to kill the man. And he tried. He used a gun and fired at him in the courtroom during the sentencing. He almost succeeded but the shot didn't kill the man. The father was then himself sentenced to prison."

"And because the father chose vengeance he left his wife alone to care for their two other children for five years. And nothing changed for the driver. He went to prison and did his time just as he would have if the father hadn't done what he did. It may be easier to hate than to forgive. Or at least it feels like it is but I hope that we can learn something from this story. I really do."

After the reverend's passionate sermon, hymns were sung and he spoke more about their close-knit community and 'loving thy neighbor'. Greene found it all rather monotonous, but she was glad she went. She wasn't religious - she grew up with it but it never took to her or maybe she never took to it - but she always wanted to show support of Paul's faith, even if she thought him overly-pious at times. At the end, after most had left, Greene stood on the grass with Alex and they waited for Paul to finish talking with the reverend. They stopped speaking, and they both came over to where they stood.

"I was glad to see that you here today, Meredith," the reverend said.

"It was a good sermon, Father, thank you," Greene said.

"It seems fewer and fewer come nowadays."

The reverend noticed another parishioner waiting to speak to him so he thanked them all again for coming and that he hoped to see them again next Sunday. Then he walked away.

"Are you still going to pick up Alex after school tomorrow?" Paul asked.

Greene nodded, "Yes, of course, wouldn't miss it for the world," she said. She looked down at her daughter who was looking up at her and holding her hand. They both smiled at each other with big grins.

"Great! We'll see you tomorrow then," Paul said. He took Alex's hand and gave it a little shake to get her attention. "Wanna get pancakes for breakfast?"

"Yeah!" Alex said jovially.

"I'll see you tomorrow, okay?" Greene said to Alex. She knelt down and gave her a gentle and loving hug then she watched them walk away and waved to her when she looked back.

She walked back to her car and was about to unlock her door when Mrs. Driscoll walked past with her son and daughter-in-law.

"Wasn't that a good sermon, Meredith?" Mrs. Driscoll asked.

"Sure was!" Greene said.

"Have you met my son? This is Ben and his wife Kate," she said, gesturing to the young, handsome couple standing behind her.

"It's nice to meet you both."

"Likewise!" the son said. "We really have to go, Mom, or we'll be late for our reservation."

"We're just going to the café on the boardwalk for an early lunch," Mrs. Driscoll said.

"Very nice! Have fun!" Greene said.

They waved goodbye and left. Greene unlocked her car and got in and was about to start the engine when her phone rang. It was a private number.

"Yeah? This is Greene," she said, answering the call.

"Detective, hope you're not busy?" the voice said.

"Captain, is that you? New phone again?"

"Yeah. We've got a body. Come down to the beach as soon as you're able. We're next to the tackle hut."

"I'm on my way now, won't be five minutes."

"Alright, good! And Greene, a heads up... it's a rough one."

She headed back across town towards the beach. She turned on the radio and listened to the morning broadcast.

"It's a beautiful Sunday morning in Piscator Bay. It's just gone past nine o'clock and the sun is shining and the gulls are cawing. You're listening to Pat Mallory, that's me! On 92.4 The Morning Commute. I do hope you continue to stick with me for the next three hours. Let's all enjoy this gorgeous Sunday morning, and we'll start the day off with the sweet sounds of Joni Mitchell."

She nodded along to the music as she drove past the century-old homes and vacant storefronts. The town was a shell of what it once was. It used to be the premier tourist destination in the county. It was famous for its good food, good scenery, and as the locals would say, 'damn good fishing'. People would travel from all over Maine to visit in the summer, but just like all things, it had reached its time of dying. The beach looked beautiful as it always did in the early morning sun. The sky was a bright blue with a faint tinge of green, and the ocean reflected the sky like a mirror. Looking out you could see the myriad of coves and islets that shaped the bay.

She parked her car in the parking lot not far from the tackle hut and walked over to the crime scene. She saw her Captain speaking with a small group of curious citizens who were out and about this early in the morning, enjoying the pleasant weather. The young officer Doyle was busy placing police tape around the area. He nodded at Greene as he lifted the tape for her to pass under. The beach was a mix of fine sand and brittle stone, and all manner of birds and crustaceans wallowed in it. She tasted the salt in the air. It reminded her of her childhood. Playing on the beach. A tall, lean man noticed her enter the cordon and waved her over. He wore a camera around his neck and he had rectangular framed glasses on. He had prominent features and naturally curled brown hair.

"Beautiful morning for a murder, don't you think?" he said with a grin.

"The prettiest. What have we got, Len?" she said.

He pointed over to the body lying face down in the sand. They walked together over to it.

"A female, maybe early to mid-twenties If I had to guess," he said, "she's been through something truly awful. I'll know more once I've done the autopsy."

Len handed Greene a pair of surgical gloves and she put them on. She knelt beside the body and looked her over. The girl was completely naked with bruises and wounds over most of her body. Her skin was blue and wrinkled. There were multiple lacerations on her torso. Greene lifted her arms one by one from her side to get a better view. She saw more wounds on her legs. The wounds on her arms and legs were different than the ones on her torso. Greene turned the girl's head. The girl's eyes were wide open and milky white.

"Christ, poor girl," Len said as he saw the girl's face.

"If you were to have a guess, how long was she in the water?" Greene asked.

"Uh… I'd say about twenty-four hours. Give or take."

"Was she already dead?"

"Couldn't say. I'll have to do an autopsy before I can know that for sure. Then I'll be able to rule out drowning."

"Okay. Who found her?"

Len pointed over to an older man standing behind the cordon. He was holding a dog leash with a joyous golden retriever panting at the end. He was standing watching them work, he looked upset but curious as to what was happening.

Greene stood up and ripped off her gloves and handed them to Len. "You take your pictures and I'll go speak to him," she said. She walked over to the man and pulled out a small notebook and a pencil from her jacket pocket. The man was wearing a sherpa-lined denim jacket. He gripped his dog's leash tightly in his hand.

"Sir, I'm Detective Greene. I was told you found the body?" she said.

"Yes miss, that's right, I did," he said in his old-timey New English diction as if he'd jumped straight out of a Herman Melville novel. "I was just walking me dog as I do after church every Sunday and there she was lying there in the sand. I thought she was drunken or somethin' but when I got closer I saw she had no clothes on and, lord have mercy, the color of her skin weren't right."

"Do you remember what time this was exactly?

"Got to be a half hour ago now. I don't know how long she'd been laying there."

"Thank you. Can I get your name, just in case we need to ask you any more questions?"

"Oh, no problem. Gareth O'Brien is me name, I got a business card here if you like?"

"That would be great, you've been very helpful."

He reached into his jacket and pulled out his wallet, torn and ragged, and out of his wallet he took out a business card from amongst many others and handed it to her. She held it up and looked at it. It said 'Gareth O'Brien, King's Bookstore and Emporium'.

"Ah! So you own the bookstore in town?" she asked.

"Sure do! The finest selection of used and new books, magazines, and home videos too."

"Ok. Thanks for your time," she said.

She walked away and pocketed his business card. She wrote down what he said in her notebook. Names and dates. The beginning of a timeline. As she walked back over to the body she saw a news van pull up in the parking lot beyond the cordon. Its great stature stood out among the crowd of compact town cars. She shook her head disagreeably then continued walking on.

"You get anything out of him? Did he confess?" Len said.

She was beginning to get annoyed by his flippancy. "Nothing useful," she said.

"Isn't he the bookshop guy?"

"Sure is. He gave me his business card. You know him?"

"Not really. Just the usual 'Hello, how are you today!' It's a great shop that. You read?"

"Sometimes, but I prefer film."

"So do I!" he said enthusiastically.

12

Greene knelt back down and looked into the girl's dead eyes then she looked back up at Len. "Have you gotten all you need?" she asked.

"Yes, pretty much," he said, browsing through the pictures on his camera.

"Do you have any idea who she is? I don't recognize her," she said.

Len leaned over and took a close look at the dead girl's face. "Oh… actually I think I might," he said.

She looked up at him, waiting for him to elaborate further.

"Yes! I'm certain I've seen her at Misty's," he said.

"The stripclub?" she said with a tinge of judgement.

He looked flustered and embarrassed. His cheeks had gone red. "It's not just a stripclub. It's also a restaurant and a bar… it's actually quite respectable," he said unconvincingly. "I've only been the one time, wasn't my scene. It was for Doyle's bachelor party back in March. You remember? But I definitely saw her then, she was our server."

"You remember her name?"

"Oh no. I doubt she would've used her real name anyhow."

She looked back over in the direction of the news van. She saw the reporter talking with Captain McGovern. He waved the reporter off and turned and walked over to them. His hair was neatly combed and his suit was freshly pressed, she wondered how he was able to look this presentable on his day off. The entire department respected him. They would always say how proud they were to work under him. That he was the reason the town was as safe as it was.

"What have you found?" he asked in his authoritative manner. His voice was tired and his skin wrinkled beyond his years from decades of stress.

Greene stood up. "We haven't got much to go on here. There are definitely signs of foul play," she said.

"I'll know more after the autopsy," Len added.

"Got an I.D. yet?" McGovern said.

"No name yet, but we believe she works at Misty's," Greene said.

"The sleazejoint? Are you certain? How do you know?"

"Just a hunch sir. We'll know for sure once we've checked out the place. Asked around."

"Alright then," McGovern said, "We'll do a briefing at the station first. Be there in an hour. And you, Len, get that autopsy done ASAP."

"Will do, sir," Len said.

McGovern walked away and headed back towards the crowd. Len turned to Greene. "Thanks for not mentioning me and the whole Misty's thing," he said.

"It wasn't relevant," she said.

"Well, thanks anyway. I owe you a drink."

"I won't say no to that."

"And a movie?" he asked, grinning.

"Really? You're hitting on me now, at this moment? Christ's sake, Len," she said.

"You said you liked film, sue me for trying."

"Another time, maybe." She patted him on the back and turned to walk away.

"What perfume is that? It's nice," he said.

She flashed him an almost unnoticeable half-smile, "It's just my conditioner," she said. "I'll meet you back at the station?"

"Yeah, I'll finish up here, won't take long."

She left and walked back across the beach to her car. She got in and paused in the front seat for a moment. She watched the sun peek out of the dissipating clouds, revealing the bright blue waters of the bay. A flock of gulls were curiously observing the crime scene from on top of the tackle hut. The coroner's van pulled up and two men stepped out. They rolled a gurney over to the body, struggling over the coarse ground. The police station was only two blocks away. She had time to rest and take in what she'd just witnessed. A sudden and immense feeling of dread filled her. She became nauseous. Her stomach sank. She rested her head back on the seat headrest and closed her eyes. She focused on controlling her breathing. This was the first murder the town had seen in three years, and what a horrifying one it appeared to be. She just hoped there would be a swift conclusion and she wouldn't have to suffer it for long.

She arrived at the police station an hour later. The station was a small building along Main Street with a parking lot out back. Originally the town post office. She parked in the lot and walked in through the rear entrance. It looked and felt deserted. She entered the morgue which was situated by the entrance. She saw Len waiting inside. He was standing next to the body of the dead girl, laying on a slab, covered in plastic.

"Took your time, I didn't think I'd beat you here," he said.

"Just tell me what you've found," she said.

He tightened his rubber gloves and pulled down the plastic sheet that covered the body. He pointed at the lacerations across her torso. "I've counted seventeen cuts in total on her body, all definitely from a blade, a small knife of some sort. Non-serrated. Maybe a hunting knife. And all of them were made by the same one. I'll have to do some tests to know for certain which kind."

"Christ. What about the cuts on her arms and legs? Also made by knife?"

"Don't believe so. They're different than the others. More shallow. Some clearly thicker than others. My best guess would be branch scratches, or maybe thorns."

He took a closer look at the pattern the wounds created.

"Yeah, I'm pretty sure she was running when she suffered these," he said.

"So she got away?"

"It's possible. The scratches look directional. And most are on her sides like she was running through brush."

"Maybe that's how she ended up in the bay."

"Maybe."

"Any evidence of sexual assault?" Greene asked.

"I completed a rudimentary inspection and there's clear evidence of tearing. I've taken swabs and sent them to the lab in Portland. We'll hopefully hear back soon."

"Poor girl."

"Look at her wrists and ankles, what do you see?" he said.

Greene noticed deep ligature marks.

"She was bound," she said.

"Yes, for a long while it looks like too. The wounds are deep and coarse. My best guess would be rope."

"Fucking hell, the poor girl."

"Yeah, she's been through hell. I've scraped her nails and taken swabs but given how long she was in the ocean for I wouldn't hold your breath for finding much of anything."

Greene's cell phone beeped and she held it up and read a text. "It's the Cap," she said. "Gotta see him in his office. Keep me updated with anything new, okay?"

"Will do."

The station was unnervingly quiet. Only four officers were on duty and they went about their daily routines as if nothing of note had occurred. Greene walked past her colleagues. She glanced at them and greeted them good morning. At the reception desk, a box of sugar-dusted doughnuts sat half empty. She felt like they were all sitting in the calm before the storm. The tranquil moment before inevitable decimation. She was becoming increasingly worried. The Captain's office was at the end of a long corridor from the station bullpen. She had to pass her own office. Her office had two desks but she was the only detective working there. She used to share the office with another, Detective Raymond Hickle. He retired two months earlier and they had yet to replace him. Maybe they didn't think it was necessary. Next door to her office was the break room where an officer was pouring himself a cup of coffee. And on the opposite side of the hall was the briefing room. She knocked on her superior's door at the end of the hall.

"Come in," McGovern called through the door.

Greene stepped inside and saw the Captain at his desk and another man sitting in the chair opposite him. He wasn't much younger than the Captain. Mid to late fifties, he was handsome and square-jawed with a thick stubble. They both looked up at her standing in the doorway.

"Sit down, Greene," McGovern said.

"Yes sir," she said. She sat in the chair next to the stranger.

"Greene, this is Detective Lipton. He's up from Portland."

"That was quick," she said.

The man chuckled. "I was already up here," he said in a hoarse, raspy tone.

"You were?" she said.

McGovern interrupted, "I called him in. We worked together for a time back in the day. I remembered a similar case some years back. Lipton worked it back then but they never were able to find the guy. I thought he might be able to tell us if they're connected at all."

"I'll have to take a look at the body," Lipton said.

"Greene, take Lipton down to the morgue," McGovern said. He turned to Lipton. "And if you think there's a link between this and your old case I want you two to work this together, alright?"

"I'll be happy to lend a hand… if that's alright with you, Detective?" he said, turning to Greene.

16

Greene nodded, "Of course, I'll be glad for the help," she said.

"Go on then. Keep me updated," McGovern said, waving them away.

Green and Lipton left the Captain's office and headed through the station to the morgue where Len continued with his examination. The morgue was cold and Lipton shivered as they entered.

"Len, this is Detective Lipton," Greene said.

"Oh, nice to meet you! I didn't know we were hiring," Len said.

"He's from Portland, they had a similar murder a while back," she said.

"Murders, actually," Lipton said.

"Oh, really? How many?" Len said.

"Depends on who you ask. There were three in Portland. More elsewhere." Lipton walked up to the gurney and looked down at the dead body. Len showed him everything he'd found. Lipton listened to Len talk and talk and eventually stopped him by raising his hand.

"I've heard enough," he said.

"Well, what do you say? Is it the same?" Greene said.

"Yeah… it's the same. Damn it."

"Holy shit! So we have a serial killer?" Len said.

"Looks like it," Greene said.

Lipton scratched his head and rubbed his eyes. "I'll get my case files sent up from Portland," he said. He pulled out his cell phone from his jacket and left the room.

Greene and Len looked at each other for a few moments, trying to take in what was happening. Their idyllic little town was about to change. For the first time, Len seemed speechless.

"You okay?" Greene asked him.

"I might joke around even at the worst times, but this is going to be a shit week, isn't it?"

"Yeah, I think it will be, but we'll do our jobs the best we can and we'll catch whoever did this and make sure it never happens again. Right?"

Len nodded, "Right," he said.

"I'm going to need copies of all the crime scene pictures you took?"

He had already printed out several copies of each of them. They were all sitting next to his camera on the bench beside the cadaver. He grabbed one of each and handed them to her.

"Thanks!" She patted him on the shoulder as she walked to the door. "Gotta brief the Captain. I'll catch up with you later," she said.

In the briefing room, Captain McGovern was speaking with Lipton when Greene came in. They stopped speaking and both greeted her.

"I've spoken with Chief Adams in Portland and he's agreed for me to work here for the entirety of this investigation," Lipton said.

"He'll just be your secondary, you'll still be in charge of the investigation," McGovern said to her. "What have you found out so far?"

"Our only lead so far is that the girl may have worked at Misty's—"

"Misty's?" Lipton said.

"It's a stripclub by the old port. We'll take a picture of the girl and ask around and see if we can get a name," Greene said.

McGovern nodded, "Alright, you two go check out Misty's as soon as you can. Len's waiting on the DNA results from the lab in Portland. Until then this is our only lead, so get on it."

"Will do, Captain."

McGovern checked his watch. "It's still early, might not be anybody there yet," he said. "Check it out anyway."

They turned to leave, then the Captain stopped them. "And Greene," he said, "before you go anywhere make sure Lipton gets a desk and show him around, okay?"

"Yes sir," she said. She turned to Lipton, "Follow me."

They walked back down the hall and stopped at her office. She opened the door and led him inside. "This is our office," she said. "You can have that desk there, nobody's using it."

"Thanks," he said. He went up to the desk and pulled out the chair and swivelled it around by the backrest then put it back in place. "This'll do."

"It's all yours," she said. She went over to her desk, took an empty file from the stack sitting on top, and placed the photographs inside. She stashed the file under her arm.

"Are you the only detective here?" Lipton asked.

"At the moment, yeah. It used to be me and Hickle but he retired and moved down to Tampa."

"Good for Hickle."

"Yeah, good for Hickle. You ready to head out?"

He tapped his knuckles on the desk, "Yeah, let's go."

They passed the morgue and exited the station. They stepped out into the parking lot. Lipton stood by the entrance and lit a cigarette. He leaned on the wall and took three drags. Greene stood by her car and watched him, waiting.

"Are you going to be long?" she asked, impatiently.

He tossed the cigarette onto the asphalt. Its dull smoke rising. He then skipped over to the passenger side window of her coupe. "Ready to go?" he asked.

"Obviously. Get in."

He got in and made himself comfortable. In the back seat sat a rainbow-coloured car seat. He looked around and noticed it. "You got a kid?" he asked.

Greene put the key in the ignition and turned on the engine. "Yeah," she said.

"How old?"

"She's five. Six in August."

"You married?"

"Divorced. Would you mind waiting until we've left the parking lot before we start divulging our entire life stories to each other?"

"Sure, sure. No problem."

"Misty's isn't too far. It won't take long."

They drove down the quiet streets of Piscator Bay. The sun was up and the sky was clear. It was a beautiful day. They saw people heading into town on their way back from Sunday Mass. Lipton looked out of the open window the whole way through town. The wind was cool and refreshing, and it blew his thick hair back. They had to leave town to get where they needed to go. The coastal road followed the natural curves of the hillside. Weaving between sea and stone. Misty's was located at the old port two miles south of town which large fishing trawlers once called home many decades ago. When they arrived at Misty's it was closed. It was built into an old shipping warehouse by the docks, and it looked like it hadn't been maintained well. The wooden walls looked brittle and rotten, and the neon sign that hung above the front doors flickered intermittently and looked prone to breaking. They parked in the lot out front, got out, and walked up to the front doors. They knocked and received no answer. The sign on the door said it opened at noon on Sundays.

"Let's go and check round the back," Lipton said.

They walked around the old wooden building and headed down the dark and damp alley, perpetually in shadow, to the backdoor. They knocked and received no answer again. Lipton turned the doorknob and pushed but the door was locked.

"Shit. Well… we'll just have to come back after noon then," he said. He checked his watch and it showed it was 10:28am. "Have you had breakfast?" he asked.

"Not yet. I could eat. I know a good food truck by the beach that will be open," Greene said.

"Alright, that sounds good. We'll come back after."

They left Misty's and drove back up to town. The town was wide awake and the people were out and enjoying the warm summer day. They parked not far from where the body was found just two hours earlier. A food truck was parked nearby in front of the beach, next to a small park where a group of children were busy chasing each other with sticks. The sign on the side of the truck said Hasan's Kebabs in large yellow lettering. There were park benches scattered around it. All empty. Greene waved at the man leaning on the counter of the truck. He waved back. He was wearing a white apron and wearing a hairnet that covered his thick curls. He smiled as they approached.

"Good morning, Meredith, it's a beautiful day isn't it?" The man said.

"Good morning, Hasan. This is Detective Lipton," Greene said.

"Nice to meet you," Lipton said. He gave a small wave.

"You too, brother. What can I get you both today? Best kebabs in all of Maine. I promise you that," Hasan said.

Greene looked at Lipton. "Oh, you just have to try the Mediterranean! I don't know what Hasan does to the lamb to make it taste that good, but they're to die for," she said.

Lipton nodded.

Then Greene raised two fingers. "Two of the Mediterranean kebabs, please, Hasan," she said.

"Coming right up," Hasan said. He began preparing their kebabs. He threw the lamb on the grill. It sizzled and spat. He looked up from the grill. "I saw the police here earlier while I was setting up. They were asking everybody questions. Did something happen over there?" he asked.

"Yeah," Greene said. "A woman was found dead on the beach. I can't discuss it, sorry," she said.

"Oh, what a terrible thing. Just terrible. And in this town? Terrible."

"Yes, it is."

He finished cooking the lamb and then wrapped it with onion, garlic, and feta in pita bread then poured a sauce onto them that smelled of a myriad of decadent and exotic spices. He rolled them tight then wrapped them in foil. He put them both into nicely fitted paper bags and handed them to her. "There you go, that will be nine dollars and ninety-eight cents," he said.

Greene handed him a crisp ten-dollar bill and told him thank you and they walked over to the closest bench and sat down. She handed Lipton his wrap and they ate.

"It was good timing you being up here," Greene said.

"Yeah, guess so. Well… not really," Lipton said. "My folks used to bring me up here a lot when I was a kid. It became a home away from home. I don't have anything going on back in Portland except the job so whenever I have some time off I always spend it up here. I bought myself a little house up the hill there. It's not much, but it's perfect for me. It's a really nice town."

"It really is something special."

"Yeah, truly."

"I'm surprised we've never met until now, the town as small as it is," Greene said.

He chuckled. "I don't get out much, I mostly spend my time sitting on my balcony, reading, and watching the sun rise and set."

Seagulls flew down around them and ate the stale leftovers that lay on the pavement from yesterday's beachgoers. They cleaned the ground and then flew away.

"Meredith huh?" Lipton said.

"What?"

"Nothing, just never would've taken you for a Meredith."

"It was my grandmother's name. And what's wrong with Meredith anyway?"

"Forget it! It's a fine name."

"What's your name then?"

He chewed and swallowed. "Daniel," he said. "You can call me Dan, or Daniel if you wanna be formal."

"Well Daniel, you can still call me Greene. Most of everyone at work does."

"If you say so," he said.

He took another bite and looked down the beach at the crowd forming. Mothers and fathers and their children began to arrive in droves. All anxious to make the most out of the warm and pleasant day. Lipton wondered if they had heard the news or if they even cared.

"Did you grow up here?" he asked.

"Mmhmm. I was born in the clinic two blocks from here. My mom planned to have me in Portland but things don't always work out. Moved down to Cambridge when I studied Law. But I came straight back afterwards. Couldn't stay away, I guess. What about you?"

"Born in a small town in upstate New York, then when I was old enough to go my own way I went and moved down to New York City and lived there for a long, long time. It all got a bit busy for my tastes so I made a change to Portland back in '04. Lived there ever since."

"And now you're here."

"Now I'm here."

◆ ◆ ◆

The only lead they had found so far was that the deceased girl may have worked at Misty's, the local gentleman's club. It didn't open until noon so Greene and Lipton headed back to the station to briefly reconvene with Len who texted, telling them to come as soon as they could. They hoped that he had heard back from Portland by now and that they found something that could put this whole thing to rest. When they entered the station they were greeted by Len walking briskly towards them, holding a file in his hand.

"Good thing you're both there, I've got something," he said. "Walk with me."

They followed him to his lab. It was a small backroom, hidden away, with a wall of file cabinets on one side, and a desk on the other side with what looked like a high school chemistry set sitting on top. They stood in the doorway as he sat down in his chair and swivelled around once before stopping himself by stomping on the ground. He held the file up with one hand then slapped it enthusiastically with the other.

"This, my esteemed colleagues, is a toxicology report."

"Okay, and? Have you got an I.D.?" Greene asked.

"No. Not yet. But what I have got is a blood report. Xylazine."

"Horse tranquilliser?" Lipton said.

"The exact kind," Len said. "A lot of it too. And not just that, she also had traces of ketamine, cocaine, methamphetamine, and barbiturates in her system. The poor girl was on everything under the sun."

Greene took the report from Len and looked through it.

Len stood and reached over and pointed at the blood test results. "Look there," he said. "Given the large quantities of Xylazine still in her system, I'd say that was given recently, the others weren't more than faint traces and could've been ingested last week, or even as long as two months ago."

"The sooner we talk to whoever is in charge at Misty's, the better. Hopefully we can find out who this girl was," Greene said.

"Agreed," Lipton said. He checked his watch. "Let's head back there, gotta be someone there by now."

Greene handed back the file then she and Lipton walked out of the lab.

"You're welcome," Len called out before swivelling his chair back around and returning to his work.

As they drove back to Misty's, Lipton looked through the case file they had compiled so far. It was bare. Several pictures of the dead girl lying in the morgue and on the beach, and not much else. They had no name. All they knew is she'd been heavily dosed with narcotics and sedatives and that whoever killed her was - as Lipton phrased it several times - a sadistic son-of-a-bitch. Lipton quietly contemplated the photos of the crime scene. He didn't say anything the whole drive.

In the parking lot of the stripclub, there sat a large, bright red Cadillac convertible parked by the front door. In front of it was a sign that said 'reserved', the only one of its kind. They parked next to it and they both walked up to the extravagant vehicle.

"Classy," Lipton said sarcastically.

"Well, at least we know someone's here," Greene said. "Let's go talk to them."

They checked the front doors and this time they opened. The inside of the club was lined with a red velvet carpet. The reception kiosk was empty. There was a bell on the counter and Lipton slapped it hard three times. They waited and nobody came.

"Let's head to the back," he said.

They followed the red floor around the narrow hall to the main room of the club. There were three stages, all with glistening poles in the centre that stretched two floors high to the ceiling. The bar ran all the way along the side of the room. The lights were on and everything looked clean and prepared for the day's business. The inside of the club was an impressive juxtaposition to its mangy exterior. It looked somewhat elegant. At the back of the room, there was a staircase that led upstairs. A sign beside the stairs said 'private - personnel only'. They ignored the sign and went up the stairs. They followed the hallway around and passed a large room that was lined with mirrors, and vanities covered in makeup next to racks filled with skimpy costumes. At the end of the hall was a door. Greene knocked on the door and heard shuffling inside.

"That you Freddie? Come the fuck in," called the voice from inside.

Greene opened the door and they stepped inside. The room was dimly lit. A large window to their right overlooked the stage floor. A man sat behind a desk in front of them. He looked emaciated and pale with long, stringy red hair. He was missing two front teeth and his nose was crooked. He was organising a small pile of money. She walked up to the desk while Lipton stood by the door.

"Who the fuck are you?" the man said in a rough English accent.

"I'm Detective Greene, and this is Detective Lipton. We're with the Piscator Bay Police Department."

"Okay? And? The hell you want? I haven't done shit!" he said aggressively.

"Can you tell me your name?" she asked.

"Cartwright, Errol Cartwright. This is my place. It's a completely legal business, no laws have been broken 'ere!"

Greene sat herself in the chair at the desk. She pulled out a photo of the dead girl from her jacket and showed it to the man.

"Mister Cartwright, do you recognize this girl?" she asked.

He took the photo from her and held it up to the lamp on his desk. "Fucking hell," he mumbled. "Yeah, I know 'er. That's Candice!"

"Candice? She worked here then?"

"Yeah, 'course she worked 'ere. She's dead? What the fuck happened to her?"

"We're still investigating, but we are treating her death as a murder."

"God damn it!"

"Was Candice her real name? Or was that her stage name?"

"Course it was a stage name!" he blurted. He opened his desk drawer and pulled out a large binder. He flipped through the laminated pages and stopped at one. Held it up to the lamp light. "Jessica Perdeaux. French broad. Yea, 'ere she is."

He handed Greene the binder.

"Jessica Perdeaux. There's not much information here," she said.

"I don't ask for their birth certificate, Detective."

"There's an address. Apartment two, thirty-four Parkwood Lane. We'll check it out. Does she have any family?"

"Don't know, didn't ask. She's an orphan as far as I know. Ain't no one working 'ere if they have a good family waiting for 'em, I can tell you that for a fact. Now, is that all you need? We open soon and I don't want you fine folk harassing the customers."

"I'm not done," Greene said sharply. "What can you tell me about Miss Perdeaux?"

Cartwright rolled his eyes. "She was a stripper," he said, "ain't much else to tell."

"Did she have any friends, or a boyfriend? How about regulars?"

"As long as they do their job I don't give a fuck what they do in their own time. They can do whatever or whomever they please, none of my business."

"One of your employees has just been brutally murdered. I think that qualifies as your business, don't you think?"

He leaned forward on his desk and intertwined his fingers.

"Hey! I'm broken up around this," he said. "She was a cherished employee. A great girl. Did 'er job well and knew 'er way around a dick too." He laughed and slapped the desk.

Lipton marched behind Cartwright's desk, grabbed him by the collar of his overpriced shirt and raised him to his feet. Cartwright squirmed and his eyes widened.

"You're pathetic," Lipton said, all too calmly. "This poor girl was tortured and raped, probably by someone you know. How about not being such a worthless piece of shit for one moment, and help us. If you don't we're going to start looking into this place, and I'm sure we'll find something of interest. Do you drug your girls? Do you like to make sure they're so fucking doped out that they can't say no? Huh? You fucking disgust me."

"Lipton, that's enough!" Greene said.

"This is police brutality! Police brutality!" Cartwright yelled.

Lipton dropped Cartwright back down into his chair.

"I'm going to make a complaint, fuckin' see if I don't," Cartwright said, adjusting his collar.

Lipton stormed out of the office.

"I want to apologize for my colleague, Mister Cartwright," Greene said.

"Fuck you, cunt!" he mumbled, coughing twice between insults.

"Thank you for your time, Mister Cartwright," she said. She turned to walk away.

"You know, if you ever want a career change, you'd make a killing on the stage. But I'm sure you know that already. Just think about it."

She ignored him. He was a sad and pathetic man not worthy of her attention. She walked out after Lipton and followed him outside. She found him pacing back and forth outside the front doors of the club.

"What the hell was that?" she asked.

"I'm sorry. It won't happen again."

"I hope not. We can't let our emotions get a hold of us. We have to be level-headed. You good?"

"I'm good, I'm good."

"We've got an address. Let's go to her apartment and take a look around, okay?"

"Okay. What did you make of him?"

"I don't know—"

"Go on. I'm interested."

"Other than being a pig? He's a fiend for excess. The car, the club, even his clothes scream someone who is trying too hard to elevate himself beyond what he's used to. I don't think it's working."

"Like you said… a fucking pig."

They got back into Greene's car. She called up Len. He didn't answer so she left a message. "Len. I need you to do a background search on a Jessica Perdeaux. That's p-e-r-d-e-a-u-x. Call me back with anything you find, thanks."

Parkwood Lane was a narrow and winding street situated up near the peak of the hills at the west end of town. It was called that because of the long park that ran adjacent along the length of the street. The park had a soccer field by the street and a woodland trail on the far side. Perdeaux's apartment building was a small wooden block consisting of four apartments, two on either side of a flight of stone steps. They parked on the street outside the apartments. They saw children playing soccer at the park, kicking the ball between each other and laughing. Greene walked up the stone steps leading up to the apartments and Lipton followed her.

Greene's phone rang. It was Len. She answered. "What did you find out?" she asked.

"Got the info you wanted. Jessica Perdeaux. Twenty-five years old. Born in Montreal, 18th of June 1998. No parents listed. Not much more info, sorry. She has a New York driver's license, so I assume she used to live there. I'm sending you a picture of it now."

"You're a saint, Len. I owe you one."

"I'm gonna hold you to that."

She hung up, then her phone beeped. Len had sent her Jessica's driver's license photo. She showed Lipton the picture.

"That's her alright," he said.

They walked through the shaded entranceway into the alley between the apartments and knocked on the door of the second one down. They waited and they heard footsteps coming from inside. Then they heard a woman's voice through the door.

"Who is it?" the voice said.

"Good morning ma'am, I'm Detective Greene," she said. She held her detective's badge up to the peephole. "Is this the residence of Jessica Perdeaux?"

The door opened slightly. The safety chain visible. A young woman peered out from behind the door. "Yes, she lives here," the woman said. "Has she done something wrong?"

"May we come in?" Greene said.

"Okay," the woman said. She unlatched the door and opened it fully then waved the detectives inside. The apartment was very tidy with a minimalist decor.

"Is there somewhere we can sit?" Greene asked.

The woman pointed over to the couch against the far wall and they walked over and sat down. The woman sat opposite them in a small armchair. A glass coffee table sat between them.

"Has something happened?" the woman asked.

"What's your name?" Greene asked.

"Carla Gianno."

"Do you live here, Carla?"

"Yes, It's just me and Jess."

"Do you two work together?"

Carla started picking at her fingers. She swallowed nervously.

"You're not in any trouble. It's not a crime to dance for a living," Greene said.

"Oh, um, yeah we work together."

"When was the last time you saw Jessica?"

"It was Friday last week, yes, she left to stay with her folks."

"Her parents? Do you have a number or an address for them?"

"No, I didn't even know she had family till she told me last week." She looked at Lipton then back at Greene. "Is Jessica okay?"

"I'm really sorry, but Jessica is dead."

"No…" she murmured. Her eyes welled up and tears began to trickle down her cheeks. She bowed her head into her hands and cried. Greene pulled out a packet of pocket tissues out of her jacket and handed one to her.

"Damn it! Damn, damn! Stupid!" Carla said. She slapped herself softly then stopped.

"I am very sorry for your loss," Greene said.

"I hoped she had finally gotten out… she was always meant to get out."

"What do you mean by that, Carla? Get out of what?"

Carla wiped her eyes. She put her hand up to her forehead and rubbed. She sighed and groaned. "This life. This job. All of it," she said.

"What aren't you telling us?"

"Not with him here," she said, looking at Lipton. "I'll only talk to you."

Greene looked at Lipton and gestured to him to leave. He stood and left the apartment without a fuss. Carla watched him leave. She seemed to relax after he was gone.

"Okay," Greene said. "It's just us now. Go ahead."

"I don't know what to say. I worked at Misty's with Jess. It was just dancing at first, you know? Just stand on a stage and take our clothes off. Look pretty. Sometimes we'd work the floor, serving drinks and giving the occasional lapdance. It was nothing. Easy work most days, and the money was good. But about six months ago Jess started making real money, like fucking stacks of money. She told me she was doing some work on the side. I thought she meant she was… well you know? But one day, this was back in February I think, she asked if I'd like to come along. I didn't want to at first, dancing is one thing, but fucking? No, thank you. But I have student loans to pay off and I thought what the hell! It'll just be the one time. We did our regular shift at the club then after closing Errol, that's our boss, he runs the club—"

"We've met," Greene said.

"Well… he and another man who worked there loaded us both and a couple of other girls I didn't know into a van. They blindfolded us. We drove for a long while, a couple of hours maybe, I couldn't tell. It was past dark when we stopped. We were at this old lodge up in the Appalachians. It was one of those big hunting lodges that rich folk have. There were lots of trees around, I think we were in a forest. Jess told me it would be alright and she was right at first. There were a lot of people there, rich-looking folk. Many older men wearing fancy suits, that sort of thing. Anyway, the job was fine and the money was great. I only did it another two times after that. That was enough for me."

"Why did you stop?" Greene asked.

"I got scared."

"What scared you?"

"One of the clients - that's what they were called - took an interest in me and told me that he'd like to do some things to me. Horrible things. He offered me a lot of money but no amount would've convinced me to do it. He said I'd be alright, but I didn't believe him. I refused and he started to choke me. He was drunk enough that I was able to fight him off and get out. I never went back."

"What did this man say he'd like to do to you?"

She paused and returned to picking her fingers. "He said he wanted to cut me."

"Cut you?"

"Yeah, and that he'd like to tie me down and… Jesus… he sounded insane, I thought he was joking. I laughed a little. But then he strangled me, I didn't think he was joking after that."

"Did this man ever interact with Jessica?"

"I never saw them together, but I stopped going along a while ago."

"But Jessica kept going?"

"She said the money was worth it… Damn it, Jess."

"When did these parties happen?"

"Every Friday."

"And Friday last week was the last time you saw Jessica?"

"She told me it was the last time, that she was going home."

"The man you met at the party, do you remember his face?"

"Yes, clear as day. I still have nightmares about him. He was old, sixty or seventy, maybe older. He was strong for his age. I don't know how to describe him."

"Would you be able to come down to the station soon to have a sketch done?

"Um, yeah I can do that. I'm going out later this afternoon, so I could come in before then."

"That would be great. Thank you, Carla."

"I told her to stop going, but she never listened to me. When she told me she was going to stay with family for a while I thought she was finally getting out. Poor Jess.

"I'm very sorry, Carla."

"Me too. Would you like to see her room? Isn't that something that police do?"

"Yes, that would be very helpful," Greene said. "Would it be alright for my partner to come back in?"

"Jess didn't like men going through her things."

"Alright, I understand."

Greene went into Jessica's room. It was a small room just off the living room with a single-sized bed in the corner. There were no personal photos or mementos on display. The room had the aura of a sad and lonely person. She searched the room, looking through the drawers and the wardrobe. She didn't seem to have much. Whether that was intentional or circumstantial, nobody will know now. Clothing and not much else. A cheap vibrator in the bedside drawer. Under the bed was a cardboard box hidden behind some dirty clothes. She pulled it out and opened it up. Inside were stacks and rolls of money. She thought that there had to have been at least twenty thousand in cash in there. She took a photo of it with her phone then put the box back and left the room. Carla was standing in the middle of the living room, waiting.

"Did Jessica have any friends, or maybe a boyfriend that you knew of?" Greene asked.

"I think I was her only friend and she wasn't the boyfriend type. She would sometimes bring home guys from the club. Only the nice ones. They all wanted her, but she was very picky. God, she was so pretty."

"How did you and Jessica meet?"

"We met in New York. That was a long time ago now. We were both trying to become actresses. Working on Broadway was our dream, but nothing came of it and eventually, we both couldn't afford to live there anymore. Then Jess got an offer to come up here and work as a dancer at Misty's. The money was good and she convinced me to come with her."

"How old are you?"

"Twenty-one."

"Do you have any family?"

"My parents live down in New Jersey."

"You should go back home."

"I can't, they disowned me. They found out where I worked and called me a whore. I can't go back."

"Then you should go back to New York and try acting again."

"I would love to… I really wish I could, but I can't afford it."

Greene felt sorry for her and was sympathetic to the girl's struggle. She wanted to help the girl out. "There's a box of money under Jessica's bed," she said. "Take it and go back to New York. You have your whole life ahead of you, go and don't look back."

Carla looked over at Jessica's room and smiled a little bit through the tears. "Thank you, Detective. I want to help you catch the fucker that hurt Jess, so I'll come to the station to do the sketch then I'll leave here."

Greene nodded and walked out of the apartment. She saw Lipton standing on the curb smoking a cigarette. She waved at him and he dropped the half-dragged cigarette on the pavement and stamped it out. They sat back in her car and she told him everything Carla told her.

"Christ! I knew that weaselly fuck wasn't telling the whole truth," Lipton said.

"Yeah."

"We should head back to the station and lay everything out, figure out where to go from here."

"Let's go."

◆ ◆ ◆

After Len called Greene with the information pertaining to the dead girl's identity he returned to the morgue where she remained in wait. He prepped for the autopsy. He put on surgical gloves and an apron. He put on his goggles and laid his tools down on a cart next to the cadaver. He had his phone recording on a table beside the cadaver so he could record his findings.

"I'm sorry about this," he said to her, then he began. He made the first incisions from her clavicles to her chest then down to her groin. The stab wounds that littered her body weaved an interesting tale.

When Greene and Lipton arrived back at the station Len was waiting for them in the briefing room. He was anxious to share what he found. The room had a corkboard that stretched all around the walls. Len had neatly placed all his findings up on the board.

"Looks like you've been busy," Greene said as she entered the briefing room.

"You have no idea, I've got a lot to show you," Len said.

Greene walked up to the board, and Lipton sat in a chair by the door. They both eagerly awaited Len's findings.

"Okay… so, I completed the autopsy," Len said. "As I've already told you, I found a total of seventeen stab wounds on her body. I've determined that Miss Perdeaux died of hemorrhagic shock due to blood loss, not a surprise to anyone given what we've seen. But here's the interesting part, only one of the wounds could have caused the severe blood loss. The other sixteen wounds were superficial, no major arteries or organs could have been damaged by them."

"Was that intentional?" Lipton asked.

"I would say so," Len replied. He pointed to a photograph of the fatal wound pinned to the wall. "This is the wound that caused her death. The Brachial artery was severed, but if you look closely you can see a smaller, shallower cut next to it leading up to the artery. I believe the killer slipped and accidentally sliced through the artery, leading Miss Perdeaux to bleed out."

"So she wasn't meant to die," Greene said, "not yet anyway."

"Someone fucked up, they probably panicked and dumped the body in the ocean," Lipton said.

"Seems plausible," Len said. "Another interesting thing was that her stomach was completely empty, meaning she hadn't eaten in several days at least. I feel like if they intended her to live they wouldn't have starved her."

McGovern walked in, stood next to Len, and glanced over the board.

"What did you two find out?" McGovern said. Len sat down next to Lipton.

"A lot," Greene said. "We talked to Errol Cartwright, he's the manager of Misty's, the club where the victim worked. He was able to give us her name and home address. Jessica Perdeaux, twenty-five years old. We then talked to her roommate, Carla Gianno. She worked with Jessica at the club and she told us about parties that working girls would attend."

"Any suspects?" McGovern asked.

"Yes. We haven't got a name yet. Carla told me she met a man at one of these parties who had some disturbing requests, and when she declined him he assaulted her. The man said he wanted to cut her. She has agreed to come in later for a sketch, but she seemed pretty scared."

"Okay, it's a start. Where did these 'parties' occur?"

"Some lodge, she said she was blindfolded all the way there, but she thought it was up in the mountains."

"What about you Len, what did you find? Has Portland come back with any findings? DNA results?"

"Not yet," Len said. "Should be done by tomorrow morning."

Lipton stood up. "We need to search Misty's," he said. "The roommate Gianno told us that Errol Cartwright is responsible for transporting the girls to the parties so there's got to be some names or dates or something in that office of his."

"You're right, good a lead as any," McGovern said, "I'll get a warrant for you to search Misty's. Find out what you can."

The Captain left the briefing room. Greene walked up to the evidence boards and looked them over closely as if there were hidden clues that only she could see.

"What do you see?" Lipton said, joining her.

"Nothing. It just makes me sad, the brutality of it all."

It only took the Captain five minutes to convince the local District Attorney to grant a search warrant for Misty's. There hadn't been a murder in the county for two years and they were all determined to solve this one as quickly as possible. McGovern had the warrant faxed to his office and he handed it to Greene who was waiting in the hallway with Lipton.

They left and headed back to Misty's. It was mid-afternoon and the club was already bustling with activity. The parking lot was full and they were forced to park on the street. They showed their badges to the bouncer at the front entrance. He was a tall, broad-shouldered man with a tattoo on his neck of an eagle. Its wings stretched from ear to ear. When they entered the club music was playing over the loudspeakers, not anything familiar to either of them, it sounded like the music you'd expect at a club like this. Rhythmic and sensual. Two out of the three stages had a dancer on them. Patrons of all sorts sat around the stages holding a drink in one hand and dollar bills in the other. Waving them about. Greene ignored them and stayed on her path to the manager's office. Lipton stopped briefly to watch one of the girls. She was a pretty brunette, she was topless and wearing only a g-string with notes hanging out of the strap. She winked at Lipton then continued to glide around the pole.

Lipton quickly caught back up to Greene and they headed up the stairs to the second floor. They passed girls in various states of undress coming in and out of the changing rooms. Greene didn't bother to knock on the office door, she just opened it and stepped inside.

Cartwright was sitting in his chair with one of the bikini-clad dancers sitting on his lap. He was whispering something in her ear. They were both smiling. His demeanour changed to anger as the Detectives came in. His smile gone. He stood quickly and pushed the girl off of his lap. The girl looked embarrassed and ran out of the office with her head bowed. Lipton watched her pass.

"What the fuck do you want now? Didn't I tell you what you wanted to know?" Cartwright yelled.

"We have a warrant to search this place, Mister Cartwright," Greene said.

"The hell you do, fuck off!" he said.

Lipton walked over behind the desk, grabbed him once again by the collar and pushed him down into his chair. He shoved the warrant in his face. "Can you read, you fucking degenerate?" Lipton said. "Go wait outside and we'll do our best not to break anything, okay?"

"You're insane! Fine! Fine! I'm going but I'm calling my lawyer. You'll fucking see."

"You do that."

Cartwright walked out in a huff and Greene closed the door behind him. Lipton began to ransack through the man's desk. He shuffled through the papers that lay on the desk. He pulled out the drawers and searched through the various books and knickknacks that lay within. There wasn't anything of note in the drawers except for a small pocket knife and a pile of pornographic magazines. Greene looked out the large window that looked over the stages and watched the patrons and the dancers and she saw Cartwright walk out through the crowd. A girl was walking around with a tray of drinks serving the patrons. Greene watched her smile and flirt with the men, and she saw her put the money they gave her into her bra. The men groped her but she didn't seem to be bothered by it and continued with her rounds through the club.

"I think I've found something!" Lipton said.

Greene walked over to him and looked at what he found. Lipton was holding up a small black notebook that he found taped under the desk. It had torn duct tape hanging off it. He placed the notebook on the desk. He opened it and flipped through the pages. Inside were finances, dollar amounts, and times and dates going back years. The dates were always Fridays.

"These have to be the parties that Carla told us about," Greene said.

"It looks like Mister Cartwright was earning a great deal from them too, five thousand here, ten thousand there," Lipton said.

"Any names?"

"Not a one, dammit!"

At the back of the book was a page of large numbers with initials beside them.

"What do think these mean?" Greene asked.

"Debts maybe."

"It's a start. Something to go on. This is good!"

"Yeah!"

Greene called Captain McGovern and requested uniformed assistance at Misty's. He agreed and sent all available officers to the stripclub. Four of them. They created a cordon around the club and kept all patrons and staff inside for questioning. They searched every nook and cranny of the building for further evidence but they found nothing more. Several large boxes of legal goods in the back rooms. Whisky and cigars. No contraband. There was a safe in Cartwright's office hidden behind an erotic painting behind the desk. Inside sat large stacks of money but all were accounted for in his books. Errol Cartwright spent all this time complaining and threatening to bring legal action against the department. McGovern didn't take him seriously. The little black book was all they had found. It linked the club to the private parties they had heard of.

The sun had set when they packed up and left the club which swiftly returned to being the boisterous den of debauchery that it was. They headed back to the station. McGovern had Len copy down the contents of the notebook and thoroughly go through it to try and find something or anything that could be of use. It was past 8pm when the Captain told everyone to go home. Lipton stood outside in the parking lot smoking a cigarette once again. Greene came out and stood by him.

"Want a drink? We usually go down to the Colossal Squid after shift," she said.

He threw away the cigarette, "I could use a drink, I'll follow you," he said.

Greene drove down the street to the Colossal Squid Inn and parked outside. Lipton parked beside her and the two entered the pub together. It wasn't busy at this time. Being a Sunday night most people had to get up early for work the next day. They sat down at the bar and Greene waved over the bartender.

"Evenin' Meredith," said the bartender. He was a short and stocky man in his sixties with a great beard that covered much of his face.

"Evening Roland," she said. "Can you get us an ale each, please? It's been a long day."

"Sure thing, coming right up," he said. He grabbed two large glasses from below the bar and filled them from the tap. He sliced the foam with a butter knife then placed coasters down on the counter and put the filled glasses down onto them. Greene picked up the ice-cold glass that was wet to the touch. She held it for a moment then took a sip of the frothy and refreshing ale and placed it back down.

Len entered the bar and sat beside Greene. "I'll have what they're having," he said to Roland.

"Sure thing, Lenny," Roland said. He poured a glass and put it in front of Len.

"Thanks, Roland," Len said as he picked up the cold beer.

They sat in silence and drank their beers. Their reflections in the mirror behind the bar were contorted. They looked like children. Small and pale. Sitting and drinking was a reprieve from the tiring day. Len had a file with him with all the copied info from Cartwright's black book. He had it splayed out in front of him and he read through it, thinking and trying to deduce what any of it could mean.

"So why's it called the Colossal Squid?" Lipton said, breaking the silence.

Greene waved over Roland, "Dan here would like to know the story of the Colossal Squid," she said.

Roland looked ecstatic. A wide smile graced his shaggy face. "Hoo boy, you're in for a treat," he said. "Buckle up."

Lipton sat forward in his stool ready to hear the tale.

"My great-great-grandfather, Seamus, was a whaler back in the days when whaling was still a thing round here," Roland said. "This was in the 1850s. Piscator Bay was only a small fishing town back then, 'bout a couple hundred citizens, but he was captain of his own whaling ship and they'd go out into the depths of the Atlantic for months at a time and come back carrying all manner of great sea beasts. Whales, sharks, dolphins, and whatnot. Well, one time they went out and came back not with a whale as they usually did but—"

"They came back with a giant squid?" Lipton said.

"Right ye are," Roland said. "Twas a massive one too, the biggest anyone had ever seen, It was the length of this inn and then more. So then Seamus became a sort of hero to the locals here and after he retired from the whaling business he bought this inn and renamed it the Colossal Squid in honor of his greatest catch. It's been in the family ever since."

"An interesting tale," Lipton said.

"Ain't it just?" Roland said proudly. He walked away, over to the other end of the bar to serve some customers that had just come in.

"I was kind of hoping the squid would attack the town or something the way he sold it," Lipton said

"Hey, man!" Len said. "That's probably the coolest thing to ever happen in this town, you gotta respect the squid."

Lipton laughed, "Alright, It was a good story," he said. Then he took another sip.

They finished their drinks then Roland poured them another. The inn was quiet. There was a young couple at a table nearby on a date, and there was a group of older men playing pool in the back. The jukebox was playing a mix of old folk and country music. Lipton half expected sea shanties to be playing given the décor of fishing nets hanging from the ceiling. A large wooden oar hung above the bar next to an even larger whalebone. The lights were purposefully dim to add to the gothic atmosphere.

"So, Greene," Len said, half drunk already. "Remember when you said you owe me one?"

"Sadly, I do," Greene said.

"Well, I was thinking… me and you… movie tomorrow. What do ya say?"

"A movie? Like a date?"

"Yeah, or maybe not, depends. Could be just two work pals enjoying a film, either is good."

She thought about it and took a long sip. She had never felt much attraction to Len, he was a decent bit younger than she was, but he was always kind and she did enjoy his company. She found him endearing in his own way.

"Sure," she said. "Not a date though, just a movie, ok?"

He smiled, "Okie dokie, not a date. Dinner first?"

"Fine, dinner first. You want to pick me up? Say… at seven?"

"Yes! Perfect! Yes, will do," he said gleefully as if he'd just won a prize at the fair. He stood and paid his tab then he left the pub and waved to everyone as he went.

"He's got one hell of a crush on you," Lipton said.

"Yeah, he's a sweet guy."

"So, tell me something about yourself?" he asked.

"Like what?"

"You have a kid?"

"Yeah, her name's Alex. She's five."

"Is she with her dad today?"

"Uh, yeah. Bit personal though, don't you think?

"Come on now, what else do people talk about in a bar?"

"Alright, why not? She's with her dad. She doesn't live with me. He has full custody, but I see her as often as I can."

"Now we're getting somewhere," he said. He sat up straight on the barstool. "Why does he have custody?"

Greene finished the last of her beer and ordered another.

"Well," she said, "if we're being honest here, and maybe it's the drink talking, after she was born I went through a period of… well I went through a lot, and it got real bad for a time and some things happened and it was just better for everyone if Alex lived with Paul. That's all there is to it. And I'd prefer not to go into it in detail with someone I only met today, if you don't mind?"

"Yeah… yeah, you're right, I'm sorry. I shouldn't have pried."

"It's okay, It's gotten a lot better lately. And my relationships with both Alex and her dad have gotten better. I'm picking her up after school tomorrow and we're going to spend the afternoon together. Probably get ice cream."

"That's nice, I'm glad to hear it's working out," he said.

"Now you?" she said.

"I guess it's my turn to spill, alright then. I'm divorced, have been for a while now. I'm a walking cliché, to be honest. I have no children. None that I know of anyway. I never wanted any, but my wife did and that's one of the reasons why we're divorced. I drink too much and I've been in anger management on and off for the past twenty years. So yeah…"

"You're just the average cop then?"

"Hah!" he snorted, "yeah… I guess I am."

The rest of the evening went by in a flash. They drank and talked about the work they had done. They spoke of the current case and of past cases. Of those that bring them pride and those that keep them up at night. The inn slowly became empty as people decided to call it a night and headed home to begin the new week. Greene and Lipton both said goodnight to Roland as they left at closing time. They stood on the curb and watched as nothing stirred in the night. No cars going by. Not even a cat prowling the quiet streets. They said goodnight then they parted ways. He called himself a taxi, and she walked the few short blocks home.

When she stumbled into her apartment, she threw her keys onto the kitchen counter. She dropped her jacket onto the floor and walked through her barren home to her bed. She sat down and looked out the window as she did every night. The moon high above, shining on the ocean. The reflections of the stars bright in the water like fireflies. Calming. She felt more sure about it all. More than she ever did. Even for just that moment, she was confident about herself and what she was going to have to do. Even for just that one moment, everything was okay.

II

Greene lay awake all night staring into her bedroom ceiling waiting for the sun to rise again. Slowly as her room became brighter and brighter she could make out the contours and crevices of the imperfections hidden in the white paint. Her alarm went off. She rubbed her eyes then sat up in bed and reached over and silenced it. Her morning routine was much the same as the previous day except she didn't feel the need to rush this time. She got up in her own time and allowed herself to breathe and get properly ready for the day. She was excited for the day and she hadn't felt this way in a while. She was excited about spending time with her daughter today, and later she's having dinner and seeing a movie with Len. This put a little pep in her step. Something to look forward to. She sat at the counter on one of her tan leather barstools, had her morning coffee with a slice of buttered toast, then she left. She arrived at the station at 7:30am and there was a peaceful ambience throughout. People were drinking their coffees in silence, and nursing their Monday morning blues and their hangovers with freshly baked pastries. Len saw Greene enter the station and he ran towards her.

"Portland got back with the DNA results," he said.

"Finally, some good news! What did they find?" she said.

"Come and I'll show you."

They went to his lab where he had his computer on, and already had the results of the DNA swabs displayed.

"So, the good news is we found traces of semen, see there?"

She looked at the computer but it all looked like gibberish to her. "Any matches?" she asked.

"No matches in the databases, unfortunately. But what is interesting is that they found multiple samples. And they're all familial matches."

"Christ… so we have multiple attackers and they're all related?"

"Yep, there were three distinct samples found, and all three had partially matching DNA. See here."

He pointed at the screen showing her the DNA segments. All she saw were lines.

"Holy shit, Len!"

"I know! this is a huge break."

"So, there were at least three attackers, and they're family. Okay."

Len handed her a printed-out file with the results and they went down the hall to the Captain's office and explained to him what they had found.

"Three of them?" McGovern said. He rested his chin on his knuckles and mulled the information over. "Okay, what else do we know?"

"We really don't have much to go on," Greene said, "except for the alleged parties that Jessica Perdeaux attended. We know they happen on Fridays and that Cartwright transports the girls to the location. If we can stake out Misty's on Friday, I believe they will lead us to the lodge that Miss Gianno mentioned."

"Right… speaking of Miss Gianno," McGovern said, "she came in while you were searching Misty's yesterday afternoon and helped give us a sketch of the man she met at this party."

He stepped out from behind his desk and picked up a rolled sheet of paper that leaned against the wall and handed it to Greene. She unrolled it and looked at the drawing of their first suspect. He was old - had to have been at least seventy years old. He was white with balding hair and a round face.

"This has to be our guy," Greene said.

"I've had it sent to the Portland PD and the FBI," McGovern said, "hopefully somebody will recognize him and give us a name. Until then, we need to find this lodge and we can't afford to wait till Friday so I'm going to send some officers down to pick up this Errol Cartwright and bring him in for questioning."

"Good, I look forward to speaking with him again."

Greene was waiting for her coffee to finish pouring from the vending machine when Len came up to her looking all nervous.

"Hey!" he said.

She grabbed her filled and scolding cup of coffee. And looked at him while she blew on it and gently sipped it.

"I just wanted to see if we're still on for tonight?" he asked.

"Yeah, sure we are. You're picking me up at seven, right?"

He smiled, and the tension in his shoulders disappeared. "Great! Seven it is!"

Errol Cartwright walked into the station. He was accompanied by two officers and a short, portly man wearing an overpriced suit with glasses. He noticed Greene watching him and he winked at her as he passed.

"Good luck!" Len said to her.

"Gee, thanks." She followed them down the hall. The officers led Cartwright into the interrogation room. One of the officers confiscated Cartwright's cellphone and the other one showed him to his seat. Greene went into the adjacent room and looked through the two-way mirror into the room where Cartwright sat. The suited man that sat next to him leaned in and whispered into his ear.

Lipton joined Greene in watching them. For a moment he thought he recognised the short man.

"You're late," Greene said.

"Slept through my alarm. I think I drank too much last night. How do you want to do this?" he asked.

"All we have is the book, and it's nothing incriminating as is. Everything we have is circumstantial," Greene said. "We show it to him and we show him the sketch of the suspect and we see if he squirms at all. Even if we can't charge him with anything, maybe we'll learn something new."

"Sounds good," he said. They waited and observed them.

A moment later McGovern walked in. "Our case is razor thin at the moment, do you think you'll be able to get anything out of him?" he said.

"We have to try, we haven't got much else," Greene said.

"Then get to it."

Greene finished her coffee and threw the cup into the trash. She and Lipton left the observation room and entered the interrogation room. Cartwright and the stranger watched them walk in. They sat in the chairs opposite them and lay the case file on the table between them.

"My name is Bernard Smythe, I'm Mister Cartwright's attorney," the man in the suit said. "You have no charges against my client and he has been abused and harassed by this department. I motion that he be released at once."

"Mister Smythe," Greene said, "your client isn't under arrest at this moment, but he is a person of interest in a murder investigation and I would hope that you would want him to be cooperative. Wouldn't you?"

Cartwright leaned forward in his chair. "I haven't done shit, and you've got nothing on me," he said.

"Yeah, right," Green said. She placed a photograph of the dead girl on the table and pushed it across. "Let me tell you what I do have, Mister Cartwright. Jessica Perdeaux was murdered. We know that she was raped and tortured beforehand. We know that she worked at your club, which you were very kind to help us with. We know that she and other girls, from your club and from elsewhere, would attend exclusive parties that *you* are a part of. These girls would have sex for money, which is a felony here as I'm sure you're aware. And since we know that you yourself would transport these girls to the location of the parties, that would be considered sex trafficking which is a federal offense that carries a twenty-year sentence."

The whole time that Greene spent talking to Cartwright, Smythe stared at Lipton from across the table. In the same way that Lipton thought he recognised him, Smythe thought the same.

"That's all bullshit, I don't know what the hell you're talking about," Cartwright said.

"Oh?" Greene said, placing the black book on the table. "Do you not know what this is?"

"No fucking idea," he said.

"This seems to be a debt book, with names and figures of people who owe money. We found it under your desk in your office."

"It's not mine."

Smythe leaned over and spoke into Cartwright's ear again.

"We believe," Greene said, "that this book has to do with these 'parties' that you organize. That these initials here are people who attend this party, one or more of whom... murdered Jessica Perdeaux."

"You can't prove any of this," Cartwright said.

"I want to show you a picture," she said. She unrolled the sketch of the man and showed it to Cartwright. "Do you recognize this man?"

Smythe's eye twitched when he saw the sketch.

Cartwright leaned in closer and looked at the drawing and shook his head. "Nope, don't know him, who's he?" he said. He shook his head some more.

"Just someone we're interested in talking to, are you certain you don't know him?"

"Nah-uh, never seen 'em."

"Well that's a shame… guess that's all then."

"What, that's it?"

"Well not quite." She waved to the camera in the corner of the ceiling, and a second later Len came in with a swab kit. "Just want a quick swab, if you consent?"

"Why do you need that?" he said, flinching.

"It's just to rule you out. It's procedure."

"Fine, do it."

Len quickly ran the swab around the inside of Cartwright's cheek and then put it in a container.

"Thank you very much for your cooperation, Mr. Cartwright," Greene said, "you're free to go now. Thank you for coming in. You've been very helpful."

Cartwright looked at his lawyer then back at Greene in confusion. He stood then he and Smythe left the room.

Lipton leaned in. "That's it?" he asked.

"We weren't going to get anything out of him, not without proof."

"Didn't you see the way they reacted to the picture, they both know the fucker."

"Yeah, I know. I saw. We know he's guilty but we haven't got anything definitive. It's all hearsay. We'll test the swab and see if he's one of our main suspects or just an accomplice."

McGovern stepped into the doorway of the interrogation room. "We've got his phones tapped and we'll have officers surveilling him wherever he goes. If he talks to anyone or goes anywhere, we'll know."

"You could have told me we were going to do that," Lipton said.

"You should have come in earlier then," Greene said.

Cartwright left the station with the lawyer. They stood out front and Cartwright lit a cigarette and looked to the sky as he took an excessively long drag.

"Please, Mister Cartwright, I need you to listen to me now," Smythe said, "don't talk to anyone, don't go anywhere, just go to work and then go home. That's all you need to do. Don't do anything stupid, and everything will work out just fine."

"What do you think I am, a fuckin idiot?" Cartwright said.

Smythe looked at him with contempt. "Mister Pentaghast sent me to make sure you don't fuck this up for anyone," he said. "You do know what he'll do to you if you cause him trouble, don't you?"

"Yeah… yeah, don't worry about it. I'm calm. You can trust me."

"I surely hope so."

Smythe got into his Mercedes sedan which was parked in front of the station and drove away. Cartwright finished up his cigarette and took out his cell phone and made a call.

"Freddie," he said, looking around to make sure nobody was eavesdropping, "you gotta come pick me up, I'm just outside the police station… yes, it's fuckin serious, just get over here now!"

He hung up and waited for Freddie to arrive. An old, rusted 1980s pickup truck pulled over next to him and he got in the passenger seat. Freddie was the bouncer at Misty's and likely the only friend Cartwright had.

"What happened?" Freddie said.

"Fuckin cops is what happened. Goddammit! Doesn't matter. Let's just get back to the club and we can talk there."

Back at Misty's the police were all gone. There was no more cordon tape around the club and it was completely empty. Even once it opens for the day, the likelihood of patrons coming in was slim. The word had got out about the police raid and most would be too nervous to show up. To show themselves at such a place. The place was a mess; chairs were toppled over and there were bottles and glasses and loose bills lying scattered on the floor. Cartwright kicked the chairs out of his way as he stormed across the main floor. In his office, the floor looked like it was covered in a carpet made up of sheets of torn paper. He looked around his ransacked abode.

"Fuck!" Cartwright yelled. He calmed himself and took a long outward breath. "I'm so fucked."

"What happened boss?" Freddie asked, standing in the doorway, gazing like a simple child.

"They found my black book."

"Oh… what does that mean?"

"It's bad, it's just bad. And they showed it to that fuckin lawyer."

"The Pentaghast's lawyer?"

"Yes, Freddie, Pentaghast's fuckin lawyer."

"Oh."

Cartwright picked up his desk chair that was laid down on its side and sat down in it. He laid his head down in his arms on the desk then he raised it again. "This is fine. Maybe he just thought it contained the names of the girls. No… he's not that stupid. Dammit!"

"Maybe we need to talk to the police?" Freddie said.

"What? Are you insane?"

"I mean… Isn't that what you said the point of the book was, to use as leverage? Just in case."

"Yes, but the cops have it now, and without it, I have nothing to protect me from Pentaghast."

"If you explained to the police what it means then maybe they would give you immunity."

"Immunity?" Cartwright shouted. He stood and walked around his desk and up to Freddie who stood more than a foot taller than him. "Freddie, a girl died. One of ours. It won't matter to the cops who actually killed her. They will hold us responsible. They will say we were accessories to the murder and throw us in prison. There ain't nothing we can do now except wait and see what happens."

"We could run."

"And where would we run to?"

"You always said that Florida looked nice."

Cartwright sat back down and leaned his head back and gazed up at the ceiling. "I'm too tired to run."

❖ ❖ ❖

Smythe pulled away from the station and looked at the pitiful-looking Cartwright in his rearview mirror. He drove through the town and up towards the hills that surrounded the bay like a great bulwark. He passed the expensive holiday homes that sat empty on the hills. All solemnly overlooking the town in all its beauty. The hillside gradually became thick with forest the further he drove. Pines stood high like mountains as if they were reaching up to Heaven. He drove for two hours in total. He came to a dirt road, hidden deep in the woods. He followed it down. A large iron gate waited for him at the end of the long winding road. The name 'Pentaghast' was engraved into the top of it. Bold and prominent. Smythe reached out of his car window and pressed the button on the intercom. He looked up at a security camera that rotated and looked back at him. He waited for a moment then there was a buzz and the gates opened slowly inwards. Creaking violently as they slid through the dirt. He drove down the long driveway, it was flanked by trees on each side. Shrouding it from the sun. The manor house came into view from behind the treeline. It was massive and built completely out of stone. It was a marvel to behold. A true testament to man's ingenuity. The driveway was circular with a large stone fountain in the centre, in front of the entranceway. A statue of an angel adorned the fountain. She stood in prayer, her wings draped down into the fountain pool. He pulled around it and stopped just outside of the main entrance. A man came out, he was about forty-five years old and was well-dressed in an opal Kashmir sweater.

"How did it go?" he said, almost in a whisper.

"The man's a simpleton," Smythe said.

They walked inside. The main foyer was decorated with the mounted heads of all manner of beast. Lion, bear, elk. Everything you could hunt was on display. They turned left off the main hall and entered a large sitting room. In the centre of the room, an old man sat in a chair next to the lit fireplace. The warmth of the fire was noticeable from the hall. The man was smoking a cigar and reading the paper. Smythe sat down in the chair opposite to him, and the other man walked over to the bar and poured himself a glass of whisky.

"So," the old man said, "what were you able to find out? Do the police know anything?"

"They showed me a sketch. It was of you," Smythe said.

The old man paused, and folded his paper and placed it on his lap. He put his cigar out on an ashtray that sat on the side table. "Explain?" he said calmly.

"They had a sketch of you, that's all I know. They didn't have a name. But they did have a black book that belonged to Cartwright."

"A black book?"

"Yes, it looked like some sort of a debt book - a ledger - but I'm not certain."

"What are you thinking, Bernard?"

"I think Mister Cartwright was worried about becoming expendable so he kept a notebook, detailing all of our business. There were only initials in the book next to some numbers. I suppose he'd be able to explain their meaning to the police if he needed to."

The man at the bar crept closer. "Want me to get rid of him, Father? He's always been untrustworthy. Let me do it… before he becomes more of a liability," he said.

"Not yet," the old man said, raising his hand. "We can't do that while the police have their sights on him. Too dangerous. He might still be useful for now, but as soon as we're in the clear and we can find a replacement for him at the club, then we can be rid of that abhorrent."

"What about the sketch?" the other man said.

"Must have been someone from the party. One of the girls? Hmm… maybe?" Lyle?"

"Yes, Father?" he said, leaning in close.

"I want you to find out who talked to the police. Find whoever saw me. Make sure they can't talk anymore."

"Yes, Father."

"And make sure to take Virgil with you. You might need him."

Greene waited by her car, leaning against the door. The sun was shining and it was warm. A pleasant warmth. Not humid or unbearable. Just right. She was waiting outside the Reginald Dalton Elementary School - named after one of the original settlers of the town back in 1792 - where her daughter attended. She checked her watch to see what the time was. She was early. She waited some more and heard the school bell chime. Moments later a stampede of clattering little feet came running out of the schoolhouse. She stood, side by side, with the other parents at the gate, waiting for their children. Some picked up their children and hugged and kissed them, and others greeted them informally with a pat on the head. Greene looked out past the kids and saw Alex come down the path. She was carrying her favourite backpack. It was white with bright blue flowers, and she had her Paw Patrol lunchbox in her hand. She saw her mom waiting at the gate and ran toward her.

"Mom!" she said smiling, her arms extended out for a hug.

Greene crouched down and hugged her tight. "Hey sweetie," she said, "how was your day?"

"It was good. We learned our times tables."

"You didn't?"

"I did!"

"Wow! That's amazing! You'll have to show me later."

Greene looked up and saw Paul standing at the top of the stairs watching them. He was smiling. She stood and smiled back at him and gave him a wave. He came down the stairs.

"Hi," she said.

"Hey Meredith, how're you?" he asked.

"Fine, just fine. How're you?"

"Not bad, can't complain, thank you."

Alex looked up at her mom. "Are we getting ice cream?"

Greene chuckled, "You bet," she said.

"You two have fun," Paul said, "we can talk more later?"

"Yeah, of course. We'll see you later."

Alex waved goodbye to her dad as they walked back to the car. Greene helped her daughter into the car seat in the back. She tickled her as she buckled her up. They drove to the ice cream parlour which was only three short blocks away. They parked on the street and walked into the shop and were greeted by the young man at the counter. The store was packed from wall to wall with people. Not unexpected with the after-school rush this time of year. They ordered an ice cream each. Alex ordered a chocolate with sprinkles, and Greene got a simple vanilla. They left the store and walked down the street to a large park by the beach. They found an empty bench and sat and ate their ice creams. The weather was perfect, and the cool taste of the ice cream was refreshing. Greene watched Alex enjoy her treat. She was glad to have this time with her, but she also felt saddened that she didn't get to spend more time with her, even though she understood why. After they finished their ice-creams Alex spent the rest of the afternoon on the playground while Greene watched her. Alex played on the swings and went down the slide and played with the other children. She laughed and smiled the entire time. Greene loved watching her play, just the sight of her happy was enough for her.

Paul's house wasn't far, although nothing could be considered far away in this town. He lived in a nice, modern townhouse near the centre of town. Not far from the school. It was white and had stone steps that led from the street up to the door. They pulled up outside and walked the short distance to the door. Alex rang the doorbell and the two waited. A shadow appeared behind the frosted glass window, and Paul opened the door.

"Hey you!" he said.

Alex ran into his arms and he hoisted her up in the air.

"Come on in," he said to Greene.

Greene carried Alex's backpack inside and placed it down by the front door next to a pile of shoes. Just inside the house was a hall that led down to the kitchen. A staircase leading upstairs began to the left of the front door, and to the right was the living room. Spacious and quaint. Paul took Alex into the living room and put her down on the couch, she yawned and lay herself down flat on the soft fabric. Greene watched them from the hall.

"Did you get ice cream?" he asked.

"Yeah, it was great!" Alex said, half asleep.

"We went to the park," Greene said.

"Great day for it."

"The best." She walked over and kissed her daughter on the forehead and then walked back. "I better be off," she said.

"Can we talk for a bit?" Paul said.

"Yeah, sure."

Paul walked through the living room to the dining area and sat down at the table. Greene followed him and sat down opposite him.

"Would you like a coffee? Or a water?" he asked.

"No, nothing, thanks. I can't stay."

"How're you doing?"

"I'm good. I'm doing a lot better."

"Good, that's good. Are you still going to your sessions?"

"Every Tuesday and Thursday, you don't have to keep asking."

"Of course I do. I worry about you. I just want you to be well."

"I am well. I'm doing much better now. Things are good. Okay?"

"Okay… I'm sorry."

There was a moment of silence.

"I'm going on a date tonight," Greene said.

"Really? That's great! Who with?"

"Len, from work. You remember? You met him at Hickle's retirement party a few months ago. Tall, skinny, bit of a geek."

"Oh yeah, I remember him. He seemed nice. I hope you have a good time."

"Thanks, I'll try," she said, chuckling nervously. "How's… damn, is it Geraldine?"

"Josephine. We're still together, been almost a year now. It's going really… great."

"Good… good."

Paul smiled. "Just… just take care of yourself, alright?"

"I will, always."

Back at her apartment Greene was getting ready for her date with Len. He was picking her up at seven. She was in her bathroom, dressed in only her bath towel, drying her hair with her hairdryer after showering. She was excited. It had been four years since she had separated from Paul and she hadn't been on a date since then. Maybe she didn't have the desire to. She finished drying her hair and she looked at herself in the mirror. Her long blonde hair draped over her shoulders like silk. She leaned forward and closely inspected the light wrinkles forming under and beside her eyes. She felt older, and she felt a little silly going on a date at her age. She always thought that once she was married to Paul that would be it. Starting over felt like an impossible task. But she also felt she deserved to have some fun now and then. Maybe this was the beginning of something wonderful, something she needed.

She unwrapped her towel and threw it in the wicker basket by the sink. She looked at her naked, freshly shaven body. Her breasts hung lower than she remembered and her stomach was undefined. She didn't feel attractive. Then again, she never did. She was second-guessing even going on this date. What if it went well? What if they were to end up in bed together? Her anxiety was interfering with her chance at happiness, interfering with her desire for companionship. She turned her body and looked at her side profile in the mirror. She ran her finger along the stretch marks that formed a riverbed across her ass and sighed.

She walked over to her wardrobe and searched through her dresses. She didn't have many but she knew which one she wanted to wear. She pulled out a floral sundress that she hadn't worn in a decade. It was simple but pretty. It was an egg white with yellow flowers. It had shoulder straps and it only went down to her knees. Perfect for a casual outing. She looked at herself in her full-body mirror and held the dress up in front of her naked body. She smiled at the sight. She put on her favourite pair of laced underwear and then put on the dress. She did her makeup, nothing excessive, just enough to give her a boost of confidence. She adjusted her breasts up and lowered the dress down a bit to accentuate her cleavage. She looked at herself in the mirror one last time and for the first time in as long as she could remember, she felt pretty.

She sat on her settee holding her purse on her lap. She watched the clock on her wall slowly move toward seven o'clock. Tick, tick, tick, it went. She nervously picked her nails, and she felt her breath quicken. She was startled by the knock at the door. She jumped up a little. She stood and walked over and looked through the peephole. It was Len. He was dressed in a smart sports coat and he had his hair done differently, it was combed back. He looked nice. Handsome even. She opened the door.

"Hi," she said nervously, but with joy.

"Hi, wow!" he said, looking at her. "You look amazing!"

Greene's cheeks became flush, "Thank you, you do too!"

"Are you ready to go?" he asked.

"Yes, I'm ready, let's go."

Greene grabbed her keys off the kitchen counter and walked out of her apartment and shut the door behind her.

"Where are we going?" she asked while locking the door.

"I got us a reservation at Francesco's."

"Ooh, Fancy."

He smirked. "Only the best for you."

"Do shut up," Greene said, hiding her smile.

Len had a taxi waiting for them outside. They went straight to the restaurant. It was a small place by the town square. They were greeted at the entrance by the hostess who led them through the restaurant to their table near the back. The restaurant wasn't busy; it was Monday night after all. The restaurant was one of the few upscale eateries in town. It was friendly and locally owned. Not quite a family restaurant, but they catered to all.

The waiter came over to the table and he asked them if they were ready to order in a thick Italian accent.

"Do we want wine?" Len asked Greene.

"Why not! I don't mind what kind, you choose," she said.

"Can we get a bottle of… Pinot-noir? Yes. And I'll have the fettuccine alfredo, please?

"And can I get the Risotto with scallops?" Greene said.

"Will that be all?" said the waiter.

"How about a side? Fries? Bread?" Len asked.

"I'd love some fries," Greene said.

"A side of fries, please?"

"Very good, I'll be back soon with the wine," the waiter said. He left for the kitchen then returned with the bottle of Pinot noir and modestly filled their glasses.

"Thank you very much," They both said simultaneously.

The waiter nodded and left again.

They both picked up their glasses of wine and knocked them together in cheer and took sips. Strawberry and Plum. The waiter returned a few minutes later with a large bowl of hot french fries, along with a couple of saucers filled with different sauces. Greene and Len both took fries and dunked them in the various sauces, trying each of them in turn. This little ritual made Greene feel like she was a teenager again, out on an after-school date. She saw Len had some ketchup on the side of his mouth. She leaned over the table and wiped it off with her finger. He could see down her dress as she did this but he didn't stare. She sat back down and licked the ketchup off her finger without thought. She felt embarrassed afterwards, but she saw him smile and the embarrassment faded.

"So, um, silly question," he said, "tell me about yourself?"

"Really?" she replied.

"Yeah, you know… like I know we know each other from work… but I feel like I don't really know you. I don't think we've ever been alone together for this long before."

"You're probably right. What do you want to know? I'm an open book."

"Okay. Where were you born?"

"All the way back to the beginning, eh? Alright then. I was born here, a local through and through. My parents divorced when I was very young. My mom and I stayed here, she loved the quiet life, you know? And I don't think anywhere is quieter than here."

"I know what you mean."

"My dad moved down to Boston after the divorce. We lost touch after a while. We hadn't spoken in - I think it was about five years - when he died. Mom got cancer and died two months before Alex was born... I'm oversharing, sorry.

"It's fine."

"Well, I don't know what else there is to say. I don't do this often."

"What's that?"

"Talk to people."

"I've noticed... but that's okay. How did you end up in this line of work?"

"I went to Harvard to study Law. After that, I did my police training and moved back here. I couldn't see myself living anywhere else."

"Harvard? That's impressive!"

Greene laughed, "Yeah, maybe a little. How about you? You moved here three years ago if I remember correctly?"

"Yeah, I'm originally from Calgary—"

"Oh, you're Canadian?"

"And proud of it, thank you very much," he said sarcastically.

"Why did you move here of all places?"

"I always wanted to live by the sea. I moved to the U.S. after I graduated med school, and just like you, I decided to join the police. I thought it would be more interesting than working in a hospital or some small clinic somewhere. An opportunity to move here came up and I had to take it. It didn't take me long to fall in love with this town."

"I remember the first day you started work here," she said.

"Oh really? And what were your first impressions?"

"Just a massive nerd, like huge, it was impressive," she said with a grin.

"Wow, that's... accurate."

"What about me?"

"Oh, I thought you were the coolest woman I had ever met."

"Hah! Bullshit?"

"No, seriously. I mean it! You seemed really - I don't know if badass is the best term here - but you seemed badass. You had a way about you. The way you would just get shit done, you know? You'd show up at work in the morning and they'd hand you a case and you'd just get to it and it would be solved by clock-out. Just like that." He clicked his fingers. "It was pretty impressive."

"Seemed badass? Am I not a badass?"

"Oh, you're absolutely a badass."

"Damn right I am!" She laughed and took another sip of wine.

"You know," he said, "In the three years I've known you I think this is the most I've ever seen you smile."

They finished their glasses of wine and then filled them back up. The waiter came over with their orders. A dish in each hand. He placed the dishes in front of them and the delicious smell radiated their senses. Len leaned down and smelled his pasta. Cooked to perfection. They ate, and while they ate a violinist played softly in the corner of the restaurant. Greene put her fork down and wiped her mouth with a serviette.

"I have to ask, how old are you exactly?" she asked.

"How dare you! I'm thirty-two years young."

"You're just a baby!"

"Wow!" he said, shaking his head. "I'm offended. I for one know better than to ask you the same question."

"You'd better not! Alright, I turn the big one in two months."

"Oh my god, fifty?"

"Fuck you!" she blurted, jokingly. "Forty, thank you very much."

He grinned and sipped his wine.

"So, Is Len short for Leonard?" she asked.

"Sure is, Leonard Dziedzic, nice to meet you," Len said, with a noodle of fettuccine hanging from his mouth. He slurped it up. "For as long as I can remember, nobody I met could ever pronounce my last name right - most didn't even bother to try - so I've always just been referred to by Len or Lenny or Leonard. I always preferred Len though. Short and sweet."

Greene nodded then picked back up her fork and went back into her risotto.

"I don't think I've ever heard someone call you by your first name. Why don't people call you Meredith?" he asked.

"Some people do. My ex-husband does, my therapist also, etcetera."

"Therapist?"

"Every cop needs a therapist," she said, avoiding the truth.

Len chuckled, "Can't argue with that."

They finished their meals and the waiter took their plates away. They finished off the bottle of wine and ordered another. Len filled their glasses and they both drank. They were both tipsy at this point.

"Want to get some dessert?" Len asked.

"Absolutely! What do you like?"

"Uh… how about cheesecake?"

"You had me at cheesecake. Umm… yes please!"

Len waved over the waiter and asked about the cheesecake. The waiter said there were two options, a pecan, and a white chocolate and raspberry. They both ordered the white chocolate. The waiter returned quickly with the cheesecake slices.

"This is the best damn cheesecake I have ever had," Len said, eating it all too quickly.

"Yep," Greene replied.

Greene thought it might have been the wine, but when she looked at Len she no longer saw the nerdy lab geek that she worked with every day, but a handsome man whose company she was enjoying greatly. He was kind, and gentle, and sweet. He made her laugh. She smiled at him and he smiled back at her.

The night went on, and Greene talked about her daughter and Len seemed to enjoy listening to her talk. They finished off the second bottle of wine and both agreed to order water from now on. They shared laughs and talked about passions, their loves, their fears, and anxieties until it was late.

The waiter came over and told them that they closing in thirty minutes. Len checked his watch.

"Holy hell," he said, "I think we've run out of time for the movie."

Greene laughed, "I think you're right," she said. She paused; she wanted to ask him something but felt embarrassed. "Can I ask you something silly?"

"Of course, the sillier the better," he said, with a smile.

"Why do you like me?" she said, "I mean… why do you keep asking me out and flirting with me?"

"Because I like you."

"That's it? You just like me?"

"Yeah, I like you!"

"But… why?"

"Why not?"

"I don't know. I'm a mess. I'm divorced. I don't have custody of my kid. I'm in therapy. I'm not, well you know?"

"Not what?" he asked.

"Not beautiful."

"Yes, you are!"

She didn't say anything. She picked at her fingers.

Len reached over and put his hands on hers to stop her, and he looked into her eyes. "Yes… you are!" he repeated.

The waiter came back and gave them the check and Len let go of her hand to pay. Greene grabbed her purse but he insisted on paying. Len called a taxi from the table then they exited the restaurant and stepped into the street. The sea air was crisp and Len saw Greene shiver and took his jacket off and draped it around her shoulders. She touched his hands as he did this. The taxi pulled up and they got in. They took the taxi back to Greene's apartment and they stood outside in the cool summer night.

"I had a great time," she said.

"Me too. I'd like to do it again, if you would?"

She leaned in slightly to see how he would react. He noticed her and leaned in. He put his hands on her cheeks and leaned in close and kissed her. The kiss was long and tender. For Greene, it seemed to last for an eternity. Every stray thought that Greene had vanished and all she could think about was him.

III

"This is the place," Lyle said, sitting in the passenger seat of his black SUV. The driver pulled over. It was dawn, and the sun was just beginning to rise above the horizon and illuminate the hillsides.

"How do you want to do this, sir?" the man in the driver's seat asked. He was a tall and imposing man with dark skin. He was completely hairless from his neck to his head. He wore a black suit with a white shirt, and had no tie to accompany them.

Lyle scratched his chin. "We go in and we talk to her. We need to find out what she knows and who she talked to. Then we deal with her however we must. That okay with you, Virgil?"

"Yes, sir," the driver said. He reached over to the glovebox, opened it, and pulled out a pistol. He took a silencer out of his jacket pocket and attached it then loaded the magazine and checked the chamber and the safety before sliding it into his underarm holster. They both stepped out of the car and walked up to the steps that led up to the girl's apartment.

Lyle looked around to make sure he wasn't seen. He looked down the street and he saw children playing at the park across the street, enjoying a few minutes of fun before they had to get ready for school. He quickly skipped up the steps to the front door. There was a small sign that had the number two on it stuck to the door. He looked around once more then knocked on the door and waited. Virgil waited to the side of the door, out of view. There was no answer so he knocked again, and then again even louder.

"Dammit, I don't think she's home," he said. He took a step back, turned around, reached into his back pocket, and pulled out a small leather satchel. Inside were lockpicks of varying sizes. He took the one he thought would fit best and fiddled with the lock. There was a distinct click and he softly pushed the door ajar, peeking in. He stepped inside Carla Gianno's apartment. A neighbour from across and down the lane heard the commotion and opened his door and stepped outside and saw Lyle enter the apartment.

"Excuse me, can I help you?" the neighbour said, suspicious of the strangers.

Virgil looked at the man and didn't say anything, he just pointed his finger at the man. He flashed the gun he had in his holster at the man, and the neighbour scurried back inside.

The apartment was empty. Nobody was home. Virgil followed Lyle inside and closed the door behind him. Lyle moved around the apartment like a wolf, seeking out his prey with a fierce determination. But there was no prey for him to find. She was gone.

"There ain't anyone home, sir," Virgil said, standing idle in the middle of the living room.

Lyle searched throughout. He looked through Carla's drawers and her wardrobe but they were empty. He ransacked the house, throwing anything and everything onto the floor. He found nothing. "God-fucking-dammit," he shouted.

"We should leave, sir. We shouldn't overstay," Virgil said.

Lyle stood still. He breathed in, relaxed, and took control of his anger. "Yeah… you're right. Let's go," he said.

◆ ◆ ◆

Greene woke the next morning. She saw the rays of sunshine pass through her bedroom windows and she smiled. She looked at the time on her alarm clock and was surprised to have slept this long and this soundly. She took her time getting up and getting ready for work. She was focused on enjoying the memory of the night before.

She was driving to the station when she got an urgent call from Lipton. She pulled over to the side of the road and answered.

"Someone trashed Carla Gianno's apartment. I'm there now," he said.

"Christ, is she okay?" Greene asked, with great concern in her voice.

"Doesn't look like she was home, the lock was picked. I've spoken to a neighbor who says she left early Monday morning and he hasn't seen her since."

"Okay, I'm not far, only five minutes away." She hung up and drove on. She was relieved, she thought that maybe Carla had taken her advice and left town. Her advice may have saved her life.

She drove to Parkwood Lane and walked up the steps to the apartment. Lipton was waiting for her outside the door. There were three officers present. Doyle was on the sidewalk securing the area and making sure nobody interfered. The other two were searching the apartment for clues. Greene entered the apartment and saw Len in the centre of the living room. After last night he seemed like a completely different person to her. They met each other's gaze and they both smiled.

"What have we got, Len?" she asked, as professionally as she could muster.

"Mornin' Greene. The place was ransacked, but there's no evidence of any foul play."

"That's a relief."

"I'll keep looking, the person or persons that did this may have left fibers. You never know."

Greene walked into Carla's bedroom and saw the dresser drawers pulled out and lying on the floor, and the wardrobe door bent and broken. She looked back and saw Lipton and Len talking. While they were distracted she sneaked over to Perdeaux's room and knelt down and checked under her bed and reached for the cardboard box that was filled with money. It was still there. She pulled it out. Weightless. And she opened it up. It was empty. The money was gone. Greene once again breathed a sigh of relief. Carla must have taken the money and ran.

"Good for you," Greene whispered to herself. She put the box back where she found it and left the room.

"Come on," Lipton said to Greene as she re-entered the living room, "let's go and talk to the neighbors."

They stepped out into the open-air hallway that separated the four apartments. The neighbour down the hall that had seen the two men earlier in the morning stood in his doorway anxiously waiting to be of use. He was an older man, in his late sixties. He had short grey hair and wore thin reading glasses.

"This is Michael Koller," Lipton said, introducing the neighbour. "He's the one who called it in. He saw two men enter the apartment. Mr. Koller, can you tell my partner exactly what you told me?"

"Sure, no problem," he said, picking at his cracked fingernails. "It happened around six-thirty this morning. I was awake already, I don't sleep much anymore… old age will do that to you. I heard this loud knocking coming from the young girls' apartment. This wasn't unusual, mind you.

There was often music playing over there, or sometimes they would have guests over. Men mostly, but I don't judge. I saw on the news that Miss Jessica was the girl that died on the beach, may the lord keep her, and I saw Miss Carla leave yesterday evening with a large suitcase so I just assumed she had left for good. Then there was this loud knocking so early in the morning which I thought was strange since nobody was home. I opened my door and I saw that their door was open and two men were standing outside. I saw a man go inside and I asked the other man what they were doing. This other man that was standing in the hall, he didn't say a word to me, he just showed me the gun he had, so I went back inside and locked the door. I didn't want any trouble."

Greene wrote everything he said down in her notebook. "Can you describe these men, Mr. Koller?" she asked.

"My eyesight isn't as good as it once was, but I'll try. The smaller one - that's the man that went inside first, not the man with the gun - was skinny but very tall. He looked a bit odd if I'm being honest. Reminded me of a rodent. A small face. Squished together. But he looked rich. Well-groomed, and he was wearing fancy clothes. The other man was big, he seemed like he might have been the little man's bodyguard or something. He was wearing a suit, a black suit. He was black himself, I remember that much. I can't give you any more specifics, I'm sorry detectives, it all happened very quick."

"You've been a big help, Mr. Koller," Greene said. "Thank you!"

"You're welcome, it's the least I can do. Those girls deserve some peace."

Koller went back inside his home and the detectives walked back to the girls' apartment. Greene stood in the open doorway and looked at the apartment opposite.

"Hmm!" she hummed, thinking aloud.

"What?" Lipton asked.

"Look!" she said. She pointed at the doorbell on the neighbour's door. It was one of those fancy modern doorbells with a built-in camera.

"Holy shit, good catch!" he said

Greene knocked on the door and the two waited. The door opened slowly and an old woman stepped out. She moved slowly and she smiled when she saw them.

"Hello," the old woman said in her aged and stammering voice. "Can I help you?"

"Good morning, ma'am," Greene said. "I'm not sure you're aware but there was a break-in next door earlier this morning."

The old woman leaned and looked past them at the open apartment door and the officers inside. "Oh my!" she said.

"Yes," Greene said. "We see that you have a doorbell camera. Could we take a look at the footage?"

"Oh, that thing! My daughter got me that. She said it was for my safety and I didn't want to argue with her about it. You'd have to ask her, I wouldn't know how to work it."

"I see. With your permission could we take a look?"

"Of course, please, go ahead."

"Thank you, ma'am."

Greene looked at the camera, she noticed that it wasn't an expensive one. It would likely have an SD card slotted inside. She took out her key ring. A small multitool attached. She used the screwdriver to remove the camera from its brace and took out the SD card out from the back.

"What's that?" the old woman asked while adjusting her glasses.

"The SD card. It holds all the footage. We need to search through this to see if it picked up anything, do you mind if we take it? We'll be sure to bring it back once we're finished. Later this afternoon."

"Of course, if it'll be of help."

Greene handed the dismantled camera to the woman.

Len stepped out into the hall and saw Greene holding the SD card. "Is that an SD card?" he asked.

"Sure is, from the doorbell," Greene said.

"Fantastic!" he said, ecstatically. "I'll just load it onto my laptop, it shouldn't take a minute." He ran outside as quickly as he could. He grabbed his laptop out of the backseat of his car and brought it back into the apartment. He opened it up on the kitchen counter and inserted the card. The card's memory popped up on the screen instantly, and there was twenty or more hours of footage saved on there. Greene and Lipton stood behind him and watched. Len skimmed through the videos, most of which just showed people walking by the doorbell to other apartments, or it showed the old woman's daughter visiting with her husband. Nobody else visited. The footage painted a picture of a lonely life. Len found the footage of the break-in. The footage showed the two men knock on the door. Len paused on an image of the two of them with their faces clearly visible.

"We've got our suspects. Thank God. Do you recognize them at all?" Lipton said.

"Never seen them before," Greene said.

Then they saw it all. Lyle picking the lock and letting himself in, and Virgil threatening the neighbour. The two entering the apartment, and Lyle's display of rage.

"Len, can you put photos of the two men through the system and see if we get a match?" Greene asked.

"I'll do it now," he replied.

Len downloaded the footage off the SD card and handed it back to Greene. She left and put it back into the neighbour's camera, reattached it to its bracket, and thanked her for her help. Lipton and Greene left the apartment, there was nothing left for them to do there. They stood on the curb, waiting. Len texted them both photos of the men.

"We should go and see if Cartwright recognizes them," Greene said.

"No point, that fucker won't say a word, at least not with that smug lawyer by his side."

"What else do we have to go on?"

"Not a thing, unless we can get an ID on them."

"I've only worked four other murders in my ten years as a detective here, and both times it was someone the victim knew. But the only lead we have to go on are those damned parties."

"Yeah. We know they happen every Friday, right? We might just have to wait till then."

"I think you're right. Shit."

◆ ◆ ◆

Greene was sitting in the waiting room of her therapist's office. There was nobody else there except for the receptionist sitting at the desk to her right. She was busy on a call. Chattering away. Greene was anxious, she held her purse to her stomach and focused on controlling her breathing. Two seconds in, and five seconds out. She looked around the room at the posters on the walls. Each one annoyed her more than the last. They all said the same thing: 'You're not alone' or some other inspirational quote meant to inspire calm. She thought about the case and how lost she was. She doubted herself. She doubted her ability to do her job to the extent to which she was meant to. The way others expected her to. The door in front of her opened.

"Meredith, please come in," said Doctor Wallis. She was an older woman. She had a fresh perm and was wearing a brown pantsuit.

Greene stood and thanked her and entered her office. The office wasn't well lit but it felt cosy. There were two leather chairs, one opposite the other. She sat in the closest chair and the doctor went and sat in the other.

"So, Meredith," Doctor Wallis said, placing her notepad on her lap. "How was your week?"

"You've probably heard about the murder," Greene said.

"Yes, I heard about that. You're working on that?"

"Yes."

"How are you handling it?"

"Uh, I'm a little overwhelmed, if I'm being honest."

"That's not surprising, It's a lot of responsibility, and pressure."

"Yeah, it is. It's not too bad, it's my job after all. I'm sure I can handle it."

"Of course you can. You've always given the impression of being very capable. Even still, it's a challenging thing to be that close to a murder."

"It is, but it's not really that. I mean… I can deal with the fact that a young woman has died, it's an awful thing, but I've dealt with it before. I've been doing this for over fifteen years now, you get used to it. What's stressing me out is that I'm not sure I'm going to be able to solve this one."

"How so?"

"The other times it was simple. Boyfriend kills girlfriend for some stupid, selfish reason. Almost always an impulse killing. A case like that is simple. But this one, I-I don't know. There's an unimaginable brutality to it. The girl was butchered. Tortured. I've never seen such cruelty in my life and I don't know if I can handle it. I put on a brave face at work, of course I do, I have to. But then I try to go to sleep at night and it all comes out and it shows itself to me."

Greene paused and looked up at the ceiling, taking slow, steady breaths.

"You see, that's when I feel most vulnerable. I don't often sleep but when I do I feel like I'm going to die in those dreams. I wake up and I'm fine, but still, that feeling of unforgiving dread lingers." She took a deep breath. "And before you ask, yes, I am taking my meds."

"I wasn't going to ask."

"I just hope we can solve this soon so everything can go back to how it was before."

Doctor Wallis wrote in her notepad. "Did you see Alex yesterday?" she asked.

"Oh, yes!" Greene said. A smile graced her face. "It was wonderful, we went to the park and got ice cream and just had a nice afternoon together."

"That sounds good."

"She's doing very well. Paul's doing a great job."

"Did you and him talk at all?"

"Yes, only briefly though. He told me he worries about me."

"Of course he does. He always has. He loves you, and just wants you to be well."

"If he loved me he would've stuck around."

"Meredith…"

"I know. That's not fair of me to say."

"You know he had to prioritize your daughter. You weren't able—"

"I wasn't able to be a mother, I know. But now he's moved on, and he's happy. Probably happier than he's ever been. I barely see Alex. Soon she'll be calling Josephine 'Mom' and I'll be just a memory to her."

"You can't think like that, you know it's not his fault for your marriage dissolving. And it wasn't your fault either. Many women deal with postpartum depression. It's not your fault."

The room was silent.

"Maybe…" Greene said.

"Paul may have found someone else, but he still wants you to be in his life, and in your daughter's life. That's something to be grateful and excited for."

"I know I should be grateful that I'm even allowed to see her after what happened, but—"

"But?"

Greene sighed. "This wasn't how my life was meant to turn out. I was so fucking happy to be a wife and a mother. To have a daughter. Now what do I have?"

"You tell me, what do you have? Because I bet there is a great deal."

Greene wiped the tears that sat in her eyes, ready to fall, and thought about what was good in her life. "I went on a date yesterday," she said, smiling briefly.

"That's great, Meredith. Who with?"

"A guy from work. Len. He's sweet. He asked me out to dinner and a movie. We went to Francesco's."

"How nice! You've mentioned him before, how did it go?"

"It went really well, we talked and talked for hours, we didn't end up catching the movie because we ended up talking for so long."

"That's wonderful to hear. Was this the first date you've been on since Paul?"

"Yeah, I was terrified."

"But it went well, right? You don't regret it?"

"I don't regret it at all. I really hope to do it again."

She wrote in her notepad again.

"In one of our earlier sessions we talked about your fears of moving on," Doctor Wallis said. "Do you feel it's time? That you're ready to move past your feelings of Paul, and into a new relationship?"

"I don't know. I'm afraid, but last night was the happiest I've been in a long time. I've known Len for a few years now. He isn't a stranger or even an acquaintance, he's a friend. And now he might be more... maybe. But I'm nervous. I never had sex with Paul after I had Alex. And I haven't been with anyone since the divorce. It all just feels foreign to me. Dating in general. I feel like it's been too long, and I really don't know if I deserve it."

"Meredith, if being with Len makes you happy then of course you deserve it. Your happiness should be paramount. It should be your main priority. Do you think you'll see him again?"

"I hope so."

"If he makes you happy, you shouldn't let yourself miss out on it. Don't let your happiness slip away."

"Yeah, I'll try."

◆ ◆ ◆

"Before you ask, no matches yet on the two men," Len said, walking into the briefing room.

Lipton was inside staring at the evidence board, trying to piece together the few pieces of evidence they had. They had nothing. He hadn't noticed Len nor heard what he said. He could feel his presence as he stood next to him. He turned his head. "Did you say something?" he asked.

"I haven't got any IDs on the two men yet."

"Oh… damn."

"What are you thinking about?" Len asked.

Lipton turned his attention back to the board. "I'm just hoping something will click. Something definitive."

"Nothing yet?"

"Nothing."

Len looked at the board with him. On the board were photographs of Jessica Perdeaux, dead and alive. There were also photos of all the persons of interest. There was an old mugshot of Errol Cartwright from when he was arrested for racketeering back in the nineties. Still photos of the two men who broke into Perdeaux and Gianno's apartment, and the sketch of the old man whom Gianno described.

"A whole lot of nothin'," Len said.

"We'll get them. I'm certain of it."

"Yeah, of course we will," Len said with a degree of uncertainty.

Lipton turned back to Len. "Where's Greene?" he asked.

"Uh," Len said. He checked his watch. "It's Tuesday, she usually has an appointment at this time on Tuesdays."

"Appointment?" Lipton said, in a concerned tone.

"Yeah. Therapy, I think."

"Oh, okay."

Len shook his head at the board and started to walk out of the room.

"How did your date go last night?" Lipton asked.

Len stopped walking and turned back around. "It went well," he said.

"Uh huh," Lipton said, smiling slyly. "How well?"

"None of your business."

"Alright then, I won't pry," Lipton said. He then returned to his fruitless examination. Len had left the room and headed back to his lab to work on other cases. Lipton kept staring at the board, but nothing jumped out at him.

He got increasingly frustrated. After twenty more minutes, he became fed up and decided to take a drive to clear his head. The clock on his radio had passed 3pm, and the town was getting busy with people heading home from school and work. He kept on driving until he had left town entirely. He was driving down the motorway heading south when he saw a sign for Misty's on the side of the road. It said 'turn left - one mile ahead'. He drove past but looked back at it in the side mirror and he thought about how smug Cartwright acted the three times they'd met.

"Arrogant fuck," he muttered.

The turn-off to the port was coming up ahead. He indicated and turned left. There was no traffic coming or going from the old port. This wasn't unusual as the port had become increasingly more and more abandoned over the last fifty years. The fishing industry that the town was known for a hundred years ago had all but migrated elsewhere. Misty's bright neon sign lit up the rusted skyline of abandoned warehouses and boathouses. It was hard to miss. Lipton pulled into the parking lot and then walked into Misty's. The bouncer let him pass without confrontation.

The main room of the club was unsurprisingly empty. There was one dancer on the stage and two patrons sitting around it, watching her dance. She wasn't wearing anything except for a small thong with dollar bills poking out of the strap. Lipton walked past the stage without glancing at her. He marched up the stairs and down the hall to Cartwright's office. He pushed the door open and saw Cartwright sitting in his chair.

Cartwright looked up from his books and sighed. "You again? The fuck you want this time?" he said.

Lipton stepped into the office and looked around with interest. He picked up a small potted plant on a stand by the door and inspected it. A white orchid. He put it back, then looked at the painting on the wall to the left. It depicted a naked woman from the back standing in a field amongst the tall grass. It was a pretty painting. He felt it was too pretty for this place.

"Nice painting," Lipton said.

"Yeah, ain't it? Now fuck off! If you want to ask me anything, you have to speak through my attorney."

"That's what I wanted to ask you about," Lipton said, turning away from the painting. "That attorney of yours, how exactly did you - of all people - find him?"

"I hired him, that's sort of what you do with lawyers."

"No, no, no," Lipton said as if speaking to a child. "I've seen that man before, a long time ago. It took me a while to remember exactly where. I worked this case a decade ago; A sexual assault case. And that lawyer of yours represented the defendant in it. Some multi-millionaire industrialist. You might know his name. Pentaghast. Ring a bell? That lawyer's expensive and you certainly couldn't afford him. So..." He leaned forward on Cartwright's desk. "I'll ask you again, how did you two meet?"

"Fuck you, I don't 'ave to talk to you."

"Remember the first time I visited you and I grabbed you by the collar and you were so afraid that you pissed yourself?"

"I didn't piss myself," Cartwright said through clenched teeth.

"Of course you didn't, that would be pathetic. Want to know what I think?"

"No."

"I know you have something to do with those parties, that's obvious. We all know that. So, I'm thinking one of the rich cunts that you serve lent you their lawyer, to make sure you don't incriminate them, how close am I?

"I don't know what the hell you're talking about. You 'ave no proof."

Lipton sat down nonchalantly on the edge of the desk, leaning further towards him. "We have your black book, and now the lawyer knows that we have your black book. He's probably right at this minute telling his boss that we have your black book. So now he's sitting at his gilded desk thinking that maybe, just maybe, you've become a liability. That maybe you'll give him up to save your own ass. He likely believes you're a threat to him now. What do you think he'll do? Do you think he'll have you killed? Do you think he's capable of that?"

Cartwright was becoming visibly uncomfortable. Sweat was running down his forehead.

Lipton knew he was getting to him. He leaned in further once more, "How close am I?"

◆ ◆ ◆

Greene was leaving her therapist's office when Paul called. She got in her car that was parked on the street and answered her phone. "Hi, Paul," she said.

"Meredith, hi! Alex wants to say hello, hold on a sec."

Greene could hear the phone being passed along.

"Hi Mom," said Alex in her sweet voice.

"Hi honey, how was school today?" Greene asked

"It was fun! We did painting."

"That's great sweetie—"

"Will I see you tomorrow?" she asked.

"Uh, I don't know, what's tomorrow?"

Greene heard shuffling on the other end again.

"Hi, me again," Paul said. *"We wanted to invite you round to dinner tomorrow, are you free then?"*

"Yeah, okay, sure. That'll be great!"

"Great!" Paul said joyously. *"Josephine is cooking, I'd really like you two to finally meet. You can bring someone with you if you'd like. Maybe you can bring Len?"*

"Um... yeah, maybe. I'll have to think about that," she said, feeling nervous.

"But you'll come for dinner?" he repeated.

"Yeah, I'll come for dinner."

"Wonderful, what do you say around six o'clock?"

"Okay, I'll see you then."

"Bye Mommy!" Alex yelled out in the background.

"Bye sweetie, see you tomorrow."

"We'll see you tomorrow, bye," Paul said.

"Yep, bye."

She hung up. She felt a weird mix of anxiety and excitement. She feared meeting her ex-husband's new partner but she felt it was a good sign that they were all moving forward, that Paul inviting her to dinner was indicative of forgiveness. She drove to the station and went straight to Len's laboratory to talk to him.

"Hey!" she said to him, standing in the doorway.

"Oh, hey!" Len replied. He was just finishing up organising some files in the cabinet.

"Can we talk?"

"Oh? Yeah, of course," Len said with some trepidation. "Is everything okay?"

"Yeah, everything's fine. I just wanted to tell you how much I enjoyed last night—"

"Me too," he said quickly. "When you said 'can we talk' I was expecting something bad."

"Oh no," she chuckled, "nothing like that. Um, what are you doing later?" she asked, blushing.

"I'm completely free," he said. His smile grew.

"Great! How about we catch that movie?"

"Yes, I'd love to. What do you want to see?"

"Anything at all. You can pick."

"Alright, I'll surprise you. What time?"

"We can go after work? Is five okay?"

"That'll be perfect."

Greene smiled and gave an awkward thumbs up and left the room. She passed the briefing room and noticed the evidence boards detailing the case. She stopped and looked it once over. It was endlessly frustrating for her.

Captain McGovern walked in and stood next to her, the both of them looked at the board.

"Awful, isn't it?" he said.

"What?" she said, surprised by his presence. "Oh… yeah."

"I've got an officer stationed outside Misty's. He said Lipton showed up there."

"What? Why did he do that?"

"Don't rightly know. Nothing happened it seems. He went in and left ten minutes later. Officer Doyle said he looked like he was in quite the huff."

"I'll talk to him later," she said.

"Good. Try not to let this whole thing get under your skin, Greene. We'll figure it out. We always do."

"Yes, sir. I know. I'll do my best."

Greene sat at her desk all afternoon, watching the clock on the wall. She was waiting for the day to end. It was nearing close to five o'clock and she was excited about spending more time with Len. She nervously picked at her nails and then once she realised she was doing it she stopped. Len came to her office's open door and asked if she was ready to leave. She grabbed her purse and she followed him out of the building. They stood in the parking lot.

"Want to take my car or yours?" Len asked.

"Let's take yours. You can drop me back here after."

"Okay."

She put her holster away in the glovebox of her car, then they got into Len's bright green coupe and they drove to the movie theatre. It was a small, old theatre with two viewing rooms. They walked into the foyer and they looked up at the showing board.

"What did you choose?" Greene asked.

"They're showing The Umbrellas Of Cherbourg at five-thirty, what do you say?"

"Never seen it, let's do it!" she said with youthful excitement.

"It's a classic! It's a musical slash romance, it's funny and sweet, I think you'll love it!"

"Shall we get popcorn?"

"Oh, absolutely!"

They ordered their tickets for the movie from the young man - who was barely old enough to drive - at the kiosk and bought a large bucket of buttered popcorn to share between them as well as two cokes. They took their seats in the centre row of the empty theatre room and waited for the film to begin. An older couple came in and sat up close to the screen. A young woman came in after and sat near the back by herself. The film began and the joy on Greene's face was contagious throughout. Len watched her more than he watched the film. He laughed when she laughed and he smiled when she smiled. They ate their popcorn and bumped hands often and laughed when they did so.

Greene felt like she was a teenager again. On a movie date with a cute boy. For the almost two hours they were in the theatre she forgot all her troubles. It was bliss.

The movie ended and the lights slowly came back on.

"That was great!" Greene said, still smiling.

"I knew you'd like it."

They left the theatre and walked back to Len's car, holding hands. It was almost dark.

"What would you like to do now?" Len asked while putting his car key in the lock.

"I wish this night would never end," she said sensually. "But it's been a long couple of days. I'm exhausted. I really must get back."

Len looked at her from across the car. "I had a great time. I'll drop you back at your car?"

"Thanks!"

Len parked in the empty spot beside Greene's car. The parking lot was empty, most had gone home. They looked at each other, longingly. She leaned over and kissed him. It was a long and passionate kiss.

"I had a great time, thanks for taking me," she said, leaning back over to her side.

"No problem at all, it was great!"

"Oh, I almost forgot - and this may be too soon to ask this - but I'm having dinner tomorrow night with Paul and his new girlfriend at his place and I was wondering—"

"You're inviting me to dinner with your ex-husband?" he said, with a little apprehension.

"Yeah. I know it's weird—"

"I mean, yeah, it is. But I'll go with you, if you want me to come?"

"You sure?"

"Yeah, of course. It might be a little awkward, but I really like you and if you want me there, then I'm there."

Greene smiled and she leaned in and kissed him again. "Thank you, truly," she said softly.

◆ ◆ ◆

Greene returned home to her apartment. She took her holster out of the glovebox and stowed it in her purse, then left her car. She climbed the stairs up to her floor. Lipton was sitting in the hall outside her apartment door. He was half asleep and seemed intoxicated. He stood up - carefully using the wall as a crutch - when he saw her.

"What are you doing here?" she asked.

"I need to show you something?" he said, in a deeply serious tone.

"What is it?"

"We need to go to my house, I have something to show you. It's important."

"Daniel, just tell me," she said.

"I can't, I don't know how. I just have to show you. Please trust me… do you trust me?"

Greene was unsure. She could see how jittery he was.

"First…" she said, "tell me why you went to Misty's this afternoon?"

"That has to do with what I have to show you, I understand it all now."

"Do you?"

Lipton walked past her and then turned his head back. "Are you coming or what?" he said.

She told him she'd be a minute and that she'd follow him. She waited for him to leave then she checked her holster, making sure the gun was loaded. She reattached it to her belt then she got back into her car and followed him. They drove through the town and up the hills to a fancy part of town that overlooked the beach. He parked in the driveway of his holiday home and Greene parked on the street. He scurried up the front steps and quickly opened the door. She followed him inside his home. It was sparsely decorated and looked as if he'd just bought it.

"The basement," he said.

Greene stopped following him for a moment and unclipped her holster. She slowly followed him down the hall to the basement stairs with her hand resting on her sidearm. He descended the stairs and pulled the light cord at the bottom. The basement lit up and Greene saw him look back up the stairs at her.

"Come on," he said.

She went down the stairs, and at the bottom, she saw what he wanted to show her. The basement walls were covered in crime scene photos, and evidence from past cases similar to the one they were investigating.

"What is all this?" Greene asked.

"This is why I'm here," he replied.

She walked up to the wall closest to her and took in every bit of information that there was. Unsolved cases that dated back to the 1980s were laid out in detail. Photos of dead girls much like Perdeaux. There were eight dead girls in total. Their deaths presented. Stretched out across the walls. In the centre of the back wall was a courtroom drawing of an old man. The name 'Pentaghast' was written above his head.

"You know I worked cases similar to this one back in Portland, right?" Lipton said.

"Yeah, I remember."

"So," Lipton said, beginning his explanation. "Ten years ago I worked a case involving a young sex worker who got attacked by a client of hers, not an uncommon thing in that line of work. She had knife wounds all over her body, nothing major, lucky for her. She had escaped from a farmhouse near the Piscataqua River. Local police found her and she told them she was held for days and that three men had raped and tortured her. She went into great detail. She said that Albert Pentaghast was one of her clients and she believed him to be one of those responsible."

"The Millionaire?" Greene asked.

"The one and the same. Of course there was absolutely no evidence tying him to the crime. Just the word of a traumatized pro. His lawyer, the respectable Bernard Smythe - you remember him? - made a convincing argument that the girl was just a whore looking for a payday. But I never bought it. I looked into Pentaghast's eyes during that trial. They were fucking soulless. He was acquitted, naturally. But I never stopped believing he was responsible. I got obsessed with finding evidence linking him to similar attacks." He stopped talking and took a deep breath, then pulled out and lit a cigarette. "I discovered eight separate murders indistinguishable from the girl's description of the attack. Stab wounds, sexual assault. I found a pattern. This has been going on since the eighties when Pentaghast would've been in his late thirties. When I saw Bernard Smythe sitting next to that fuck Cartwright, I knew I was right. I knew this was the same. That it was happening again."

"What can we prove?"

"Not a fucking thing. That's the issue. It's all circumstantial. There's nothing tying him to the deaths except for one shoddy eye-witness account and a sketch."

"Where does he live? This Pentaghast?"

"He has an estate up north, deep in the forest, not far from Mt. Blue."

"That's a fair way."

"I drove up there once. Waited outside for a while, just watching. It looked impenetrable. There were security cameras everywhere and the gates were massive."

"We should drive up there tomorrow," she said, with a newfound purpose. "We'll ask him some questions. See if we can get anything out of him."

"Yes, good. Thank you for listening to me."

"If it means anything… I believe you. I think you're right about all of it."

IV

Lipton waited for Greene outside her apartment building. He leaned against his car, tapping the roof incessantly. She came out wearing her grey work suit and she carried a look of great determination. She had a purposeful stride and a reinvigorated outlook on the case.

"Good morning," she said, "you ready to head off?"

"Yeah, let's get going," he said.

They got in and began their journey north. Lipton drove quietly, with a piercing focus. He didn't say much of anything along the way. If anything at all. Greene looked out the window most of the way, just admiring the countryside. Quiet contemplation. They passed hillsides and lakes and great rivers that stretched far across the state. There was a field full of cows that seemed to watch them as they drove past. It was truly beautiful country. They travelled up the 275 onto the 95 and continued up through Augusta. Greene opened the window and allowed herself to bask in the wind. Her hair flowed with the breeze like tall grass. Once they had passed Wilton they knew they were close. There was a small, almost unnoticeable turnoff just before the entrance to the state park. It was a long dirt road that led deep into the surrounding woodland. At the end of the road was the massive iron gate. It was old and beginning to rust in its corners.

"Here we are," Lipton said.

Greene leaned forward and looked up at the gate through the windscreen. It towered above them. The engraved name stood out. Lipton pulled forward slowly up to the gate intercom then he wound down his window and leaned out and pressed the button. They waited for a response.

"Yes? What do you want?" said a hard and impatient voice.

"Hi," Lipton said, "I'm Detective Lipton and this is Detective Greene. We're with the Piscator Bay Police Department. We would like to speak to Mr. Pentaghast, please?"

"Hold on a moment," the voice said.

There was silence for a couple of minutes, then the voice came back. "Please enter," he said.

There was a loud buzz and the gate opened slowly, it looked heavy and it made a deep creaking sound when it moved. They drove up the rest of the driveway, up to the manor house. Its stone construction was a stark contrast to its surroundings. The woodland that surrounded the entire house trapped it in an eternal shade. They pulled around the fountain and slowed to the entrance. A man waited for them by the entranceway. He was a short, middle-aged man. He wore a tuxedo and had a thin moustache. They parked in front of the man.

"Let's not do anything stupid," Greene said.

"I'll be polite, don't worry," Lipton said.

They exited the car and walked up to the man.

"Good morning," The man said. "Please, follow me."

The man turned and they followed him into the house. As they entered, Greene looked up at the unreachable ceiling. It was a beamed ceiling. She noticed a small bird fluttering around up there, floating from beam to beam. The man - who Greene suspected was the butler - led them down the main hall to the back of the house. They followed the wooden floor and exited a rear door into the back garden. The gardens were lush and vibrantly coloured with all manner of native trees and flowers. They walked through the gardens to a large greenhouse at the back. The man stopped at the glass door that led inside.

"Please, Mr. Pentaghast is waiting for you," he said. He made a gesture for them to go on through.

Lipton went in first and Greene followed closely. Every type of exotic plant imaginable was in there. From tall palm trees that reached the ceiling, down to roses, orchids, and carnations. It was a beautiful and peaceful place. There was a fine mist that filled the room and it was warmer in there than they had ever experienced. Humid and suffocating. At the back of the room, an old man was trimming a white rose bush. They approached him.

"I remember you, Detective Lipton," Pentaghast said without turning from his roses.

"I'd hope so," Lipton said. He pushed the branches and leaves that hung down out of his way as he walked closer up to Pentaghast.

"Who's your friend?" Pentaghast asked.

Greene followed Lipton to the back and stood beside him and answered his question herself. "Detective Greene," she said, "we have some questions for you Mr. Pentaghast."

"Of course you do, why else would you come all this way?" He put down his pruning shears and turned to face the detectives. "Shall we take this to the conservatory? There we can sit comfortably."

Pentaghast shuffled past them and proceeded to leave the greenhouse. They followed him back towards the manor. To the right of the back doors was an entrance to the conservatory. There were chairs and a table in the centre, and in the corner was a telescope pointing to the sky through the clear glass roof. A tall birdcage sat by the wall and inside were two lovebirds, perched on top of a plastic branch. Pentaghast sat in one of the chairs and waited for the detectives to sit themselves. Once they were seated he gestured for the butler to come over.

"Adrian," he said, "please bring some water for the detectives, they've had quite the journey. And get me a scotch. Thank you."

The butler nodded and left.

"So," Pentaghast said, clapping his hands once as if to remind them why they came. "You said you wished to ask me some questions?"

"That's right," Lipton said sternly.

"Well... go ahead."

"Tell me, Albert, how would someone like you know Errol Cartwright?"

"Who?"

"Errol Cartwright."

Pentaghast shook his head. "I'm not familiar with that name, detective," he said.

"Cartwright is a club owner. He owns Misty's, you know it?"

"No, can't say I do. What kind of place is it?"

Greene chimed in, "It's a stripclub," she said.

"Oh." Pentaghast laughed. "I'm afraid I'm a bit old for places such as that," he said.

"Really?" Lipton said. "Can you then explain to me how this lowlife piece of shit—"

"Language detective," Pentaghast interrupted. "Please... have some decorum. You are a professional, after all."

Lipton gritted his teeth. His foot tapped relentlessly on the stone floor below. Before he could continue his questioning, the butler came back into the conservatory, carrying a tray of drinks. He handed Greene and Lipton both their glasses of ice-cold water and then he handed Pentaghast a small glass of scotch.

"Will there be anything else, sir?" the butler asked.

"No, thank you, Adrian. That'll be all."

"Sir."

The butler left again and the room was quiet while everyone had a drink. The silence was broken by the birds chirping.

"Would you like to repeat the question, detective?" Pentaghast said.

"Why would Errol Cartwright, a stripclub owner, have the same lawyer as you?"

"Who, Bernard? Hark! Bernard's a freelancer, he represents many people, high and low. You think because this Cartwright fellow and I share a lawyer we must be, what? Compatriots of some kind? A ridiculous assumption."

"You know a girl was found murdered over in Piscator Bay, right?"

"Yes, I heard about that. A tragic thing."

"Well, she worked for Cartwright. She was a dancer. But here's what's more interesting than just you and Cartwright sharing a lawyer; The manner in which she was murdered."

"Oh… How so?"

"She was stabbed, repeatedly. Raped and tortured, then stabbed to death. Eerily similar to the murder of Caitlyn Sommers. You remember her?"

Pentaghast's face turned red and his friendly, genteel demeanour became hostile. "I was acquitted of that, or don't you remember?" he said.

"Bit of a coincidence that the lawyer who got you acquitted is now here, representing a person of interest in a similar murder, don't you think?"

"No, detective, I don't. People die every day. Many of them in similar circumstances. It doesn't always mean they're connected."

They stared at each other for a moment.

Pentaghast turned to Greene, "Don't you speak?" he said condescendingly.

Greene shrugged. "I thought he was doing just fine," she said.

Lipton reached into his coat pocket and pulled out a large folded piece of paper. He unfolded it and placed it on the table in front of Pentaghast. It was a copy of the sketch that Carla Gianno did of the old man. "Looks a lot like you, don't you think?" he said.

"What is that?" Pentaghast asked, leaning forward to see more clearly.

"It's a police sketch, from an eyewitness. The spitting image of you, isn't it."

Pentaghast finished his scotch then stood up. "Unless you have some actual evidence that ties me to these crimes that isn't just some crude drawing, we're done here. If you wish to ask me any further questions, you can contact my lawyer. You know who he is. Now, if you please, with respect, get the hell out." He walked out of the conservatory and headed back towards his greenhouse.

The butler stood in the doorway that led back into the house and gestured for them to go.

They walked back through the house to the front door. The butler kept pace with them, watching them like an owl. Greene had already gone outside, but Lipton stopped and looked at a framed photograph sitting on a small cabinet in the hall, beside the foyer. The photo was of Pentaghast and two other men sitting on a dock, holding up the fish they'd caught. All looking proud. Lipton recognised the other men. Bernard Smythe stood to Pentaghast's left, while the man on his right was the same man who broke in and ransacked Perdeaux and Gianno's apartment.

"Who is that?" Lipton asked the butler, pointing at the unknown man.

"That sir, is Lyle, Mr. Pentaghast's son," the butler said, in a dismissive tone.

"Interesting, thank you."

They left the house and returned to Lipton's car. The butler watched them get in and didn't turn his gaze from them for a second.

"Did you see the picture in the hall?" Lipton asked.

"I did…" Greene replied.

"I asked Jeeves and he said the other man is Lyle Pentaghast, Albert's son. The same man from the door cam."

"We'll bring up his file back at the station then we can get a warrant. Bring him in for questioning."

"We're so fucking close to ending this," Lipton said, with a smile.

"Let's get back first."

"Right," Lipton said. He started the engine and they pulled around the circular motor court, passed the fountain, and drove back down the long driveway. The stone angel watched them as they went. Lipton checked the rearview mirror and saw the butler step back inside. He was relieved, he may not have found definitive proof of Pentaghast's involvement but the knowledge that the son was gave him the feeling that he was nearing the end.

On the way back to town they stopped off at a truck stop for something to eat. It was deserted except for the staff and one trucker sitting at the counter eating a sandwich with a coffee. They sat at a booth by the window and the woman at the counter came over to take their orders. She was middle-aged and seemed to have a permanent smile attached.

"What can I get you both?" she asked.

Lipton ordered the eggs and bacon, and Greene ordered one of the chicken burgers. They both ordered coffee. A different, and much younger waitress came back with their drinks.

They didn't speak much. They just waited. Greene watched the cook through the open window behind the counter. He was a tall and hunched man busy frying the bacon on the grill. Smoke rising up around him. A truck pulled up outside and an older man stepped out and came into the diner. He waved and said good morning to all three of the staff and sat himself at the counter. From the conversation Greene overheard, the staff were all related, a husband and wife and their daughter.

The young server brought their plates over and they thanked her and enjoyed their breakfasts before returning to the road. Greene was thankful for small reprieves such as this. A brief moment of peace between the stresses of work and life.

◆ ◆ ◆

"You've got to be kidding me?" McGovern said. "You want me to sign an arrest warrant for Lyle Pentaghast, the son of Albert Pentaghast? Are you both off your nut?"

"Sir," Greene said, standing in front of the captain's desk. "We have footage of him breaking into Perdeaux and Gianno's apartment. That's got to be enough for an arrest."

"Yes, I know it is. Damn it. Alright then, I'll sign it, but you know that Pentaghast owns half this damn state. He won't take this lightly. He'll bring all his lawyers down on us. He's got friends in the State Senate."

"I'm aware of his reach, sir. I'm prepared to take whatever shit comes my way, if I have to."

"Alright, I just hope you're right about this."

"I am," she said confidently.

McGovern signed the warrant. "I'll send this over to the district attorney's office and if he gives the okay, I'll let you know, okay?" he said.

"Thank you, Captain."

She left his office and walked over to Lipton who was busy getting a coffee from the machine in the hall. He sipped his coffee and turned to her.

"Well?" he said.

"It's up to the district attorney, we'll find out soon."

"Alright then. That's good. What do we do until then?"

"Not much we can do except wait."

They waited until the clock struck four. How quick the day had gone. Lipton was on his fifth cup of coffee for the day. He was already agitated but now he was aching for something - or anything - to happen.

Captain McGovern entered Greene's office. He was holding a file. "Judge granted the warrant, I want you to bring him in. Just make sure it all goes smooth," he said.

Both Greene and Lipton leapt up out of their seats and began to leave with great haste.

McGovern stopped them before they left. "Wait a second, I'm not done. I just heard from Officer Doyle - he's stationed outside Misty's. He saw your man enter only a short minute ago, go get him."

◆ ◆ ◆

Cartwright was standing at the bar pouring drinks when Lyle approached him with Virgil in tow.

"Get me a beer," Lyle ordered.

Cartwright grabbed a bottle of lager from the fridge underneath the bar, popped the cap, and handed it to him. Cartwright gestured to Virgil if he'd like something, but he shook his head.

Lyle drank. He looked around at the sparsely attended club. The crowd would eventually show, but for now, it was quiet, save for the booming music.

"We need to talk. Somewhere private," Lyle said loudly, attempting to be heard over the loud club music playing over the speakers.

"Yeah, man. No problem. Follow me."

Cartwright walked out from behind the bar, and they went across the main floor toward the staircase that led to his office. He pivoted to the door next to the stairs. The sign on the door read 'storage', and the door was made of a thick mahogany. He detached the key ring from his belt and flipped through the keys until he found the right one. He unlocked the door and the two entered. Virgil remained outside, standing guard.

The room was dim, lit only by a single bulb hanging from the ceiling. The room was filled with open crates of booze, resting carefully upon piles of straw. And massive locked containers surrounded them, filled with god-knows-what.

"Interesting collection," Lyle said.

"It's just supplies for the pub."

"Of course, what else?"

"So, what did you want to discuss?"

"I'm concerned. As is my father. This damned business with the dead girl is becoming a hindrance and we need it to be sorted quick."

"I completely agree… how do we do that?"

"Well, we have a couple of choices," Lyle said. He stepped up close to Cartwright, towering over the puny Anglo. "My father asked me to kill you, and frame you for the murder—"

"Woah! B-but I didn't do it," Cartwright whined.

"No shit, we both know that. But you're already a person of interest to the police and you're likely to end up in prison soon anyhow, so what would be the difference?"

"They won't believe it."

"You underestimate us, Errol."

"And the other choice?"

"You don't die. Bully for you. Instead, you turn yourself in and confess to everything."

"And why the hell would I do that?"

"So you can live. Obviously. Do try to follow along. In return, I will personally guarantee your comfort. You'll live like a king. I'll take control of your club and everything will be as it should be."

"How do you know that you're not a suspect? Huh? How do you know the police aren't already hunting you?"

Lyle didn't respond. He just stared at him with a dead expression, never blinking.

"Of course I haven't said anything to them," Cartwright said. "I would never, you can count on me, always. I'm no rat."

"So you agree then? I would prefer not to kill you."

"No! I don't agree to your fucking plan," Cartwright belted. He pointed his finger at Lyle's chest. "If you did kill me, do you seriously think I don't 'ave contingencies in place? Yeah! Everything I know about you and your father will become public knowledge. You'll be fuckin' shunned. A pathetic joke of a family, laughed at by those reading the morning paper. And do you think I don't 'ave friends that will fuckin' kill you if you harm me? I'm not someone you fuck with!"

Lyle's eyes widened with surprise. "Wow!" he said. "The little dog's got bite."

Cartwright nodded.

Lyle swiftly raised his right hand up and backhanded Cartwright across the jaw with his fist. The club-owner fell to his knees clutching his bruised cheek. Lyle leaned down and grabbed him by the throat and held him down and squeezed. Cartwright's face turned a reddish hue he'd never seen before. He began to drool blood. His arms thrashing. Lyle kept squeezing until Virgil stormed in and locked the door behind him.

"We have to leave, now!" Virgil said.

A loud bang at the door followed.

◆ ◆ ◆

They took Greene's car and quickly drove down to Misty's. It had started to rain lightly. Clouding over. They parked in the space beside the club entrance that was reserved for VIP guests. Officer Doyle was waiting for them next to the entrance. He was a young Texan and had only been at the job for a short few months. Everybody liked him. He was green but eager to impress. He gave them a wave and walked up to the driver's side window.

"He's been in there for about twenty minutes," Doyle said.

Greene and Lipton got out of the car. She grabbed her portable radio from on top of the dashboard and attached it to her belt, next to her sidearm.

"Was he alone?" Greene asked.

"No, some big fella was with him, looked like security. A bodyguard."

"Alright," she said, "you stay here and keep watch the on door. We'll go in and ask him nicely to come with us to the station."

"Sure thing, detective," Doyle said. He walked back and stood vigilantly on guard by the front entrance.

Greene and Lipton walked up to the entrance, the bouncer didn't obstruct their path. There was a flash of lightning in the sky from beyond the bay, and thunder roared in the distance.

"Looks like a storm's coming," Lipton said, staring up at the darkening sky.

They entered the club, it was near empty just as it had been every other time they'd been there before. They looked around the main floor for Lyle but couldn't see him. They stood by the bar, trying to remain covert. The music was so loud they couldn't hear themselves think. They recognised the other man at the other end of the building. Virgil was standing by the door that led to the back of the building. He had already clocked the detectives as they entered and was watching them. They left the bar and approached him slowly. Greene walked ahead and had her badge out ready to be shown. Lipton followed behind her and kept his hand rested on his sidearm. Virgil didn't move nor did he react.

"Police!" she said, holding up her badge. "We have a warrant to take Lyle Pentaghast in for questioning. Is he in there?"

Virgil didn't say a word, he glanced back at the door behind him and then looked back at the detectives.

"Open the door, asshole!" Lipton ordered.

Virgil stood still, staring at him. A slight grin. There was a moment of silence, it was so silent you could hear their hearts beat. Virgil quickly sprung from his inertness and pushed Greene backwards into Lipton. The two of them lost their footing and stumbled back. He pulled the door open behind him and entered and closed it. There was the loud thud of a bolt latching.

Lipton regained his balance, unholstered his weapon and ran at the door. He thrust his foot forward and kicked the door. It was a reinforced door and it took him three attempts to finally barge it open. He aimed his weapon and moved into the back room. Greene followed him, with her weapon drawn. They could hear movement ahead of them.

Cartwright was on his knees with one hand up and the other massaging his neck, "I haven't done shit, he tried to fuckin' kill me," he said. He took a painful breath and pointed to the rear of the dark room. "They went that way."

Greene unclipped her radio from her belt. "I'm gonna call for backup," she said. "This is Greene, requesting uniformed assistance at Misty's, suspect on the run. I repeat, suspect is on the run."

Officer Doyle heard the call and radioed back. He unholstered his sidearm and headed around to the side of the club.

The back room was dark and they followed it to a staircase at the rear that led down into further darkness. They carefully moved to the staircase and looked down over the railing and saw the two men reach the bottom.

"Hey! Stop! Police!" Lipton shouted.

Virgil stopped at the bottom and looked up at them. He pulled out his pistol and fired two shots up at them. The bullets hit the railing, ricocheting across the room.

Cartwright laid himself flat on his stomach and covered his head.

Lipton fired three shots back but Virgil had already disappeared from sight. They descended the stairs slowly and carefully with their weapons raised out in front of them. At the bottom of the staircase, they took cover behind the thick stone walls on either side of the exit. The stairs had led to the beginning of a long corridor, an old smuggling tunnel from the prohibition era that led out to the ocean. They peered down it and couldn't see anyone.

"If anyone can hear this," Greene said, into her radio. "The two suspects have gone out the back, I repeat, they've fled out the back. They're armed and dangerous."

They continued down the tunnel. It was dark and they both turned on their flashlights. They heard the sounds of water dripping above them and footsteps could be heard ahead of them. There was no light down there except from their flashlights. They reached a corner and as they turned down into the next hall, Virgil fired two more shots at them, the bullets hit the corner of the wall, one lodging itself in the stone and the other bursting through it and narrowly missing Lipton's head. Both Lipton and Greene returned fire and a yell was heard. The two of them continued down the tunnel and reached another corner, this was the last one, at the far end was a door leading outside.

Virgil was limping ahead of them, and gripping his leg with his free hand. Lyle had already reached the door.

"Come on," Lyle yelled, frantically waving to him. "Hurry up!"

Virgil looked back at the detectives getting nearer. He sped up and lost his footing, falling to the floor. He looked up at Lyle. "Go! Now!" he said.

Lyle hesitated, then he saw the detectives coming for him and made his choice. He opened the door and exited the tunnel. He closed the door behind him and looked around and saw a two-by-four plank of wood lying on the wet concrete. He picked it up and wedged it between the ground and the door handle, locking them all in.

Virgil stood and leaned against the wall. He turned towards the approaching detectives. He raised his weapon and fired at them. The suppressed gunshots sounded as loud as any other in the cramped tunnel. He was losing a lot of blood, becoming faint, and his aim was poor as a result.

Greene and Lipton threw themselves to either side of the tunnel to avoid the gunfire. They fired back. They hit their target. Greene fired three shots, while Lipton emptied his magazine into the man and kept firing even when all he heard were clicks.

Virgil slid down the wall, leaving a trail of blood behind him. His head crashed against the concrete floor with tremendous force.

They approached him with their weapons still drawn. A pool of blood was forming around his still body. Lipton reloaded his gun and charged at the door with all his might, but it wouldn't budge.

◆ ◆ ◆

Lyle heard the banging against the door and quickly walked away. He was at the edge of the old port, half a mile away from Misty's. He was standing next to a canal on the sewer level below the warehouses. It was completely deserted. He stopped to take a breath and he felt the rain fall on his head. He looked up at the dark sky then he continued on. He walked up the narrow steps that led back up and he walked around the three large warehouses that stood between him and Misty's where he had parked his car. He passed the backdoor into the club and reached a spot where he could see into the parking lot. He saw five police cars in the lot, all with their lights flashing brightly in the gloom of the evening. The neighbouring buildings were lit up in shades of red and blue.

"Fuck," he muttered. Breathing heavily. He banged his head lightly against the wall. He had a boat moored at a marina not far from there. Walking distance. He turned back to head towards it when he saw a man walking towards him, coming out from behind the nearest warehouse. He knew he couldn't turn back so he kept moving forward.

Officer Doyle was patrolling the perimeter of the club when he spotted a man in the shadows behind the warehouse beside Misty's. He held his firearm up.

"Police officer, identify yourself!" he shouted into the dark.

"Officer, p-please help me, I-I was attacked," Lyle said, with an intentional quiver in his voice. He held the back of his head as if it were injured, and moved towards the officer.

"Where? And who hurt you?" asked Doyle.

Lyle pointed behind Doyle. "J-Just over there," he said.

Doyle turned to look. A great error in judgement. Lyle lunged at him from behind. He grabbed Doyle's pistol with one hand and wrapped his other one tightly around the unsuspecting officer's neck. He pulled him to the side of the alley and threw him into the wall.

Doyle released his grip on the gun, and he fell to the ground. He attempted to stand.

Lyle kicked the gun away from them and then he kicked Doyle in the stomach and the chest, again and again until he was no longer trying to get up.

"I am sorry about this, truly," Lyle said. He grabbed Doyle by the throat and pushed him back so his head was firmly against the concrete wall. He then pulled out a small, thin blade from his belt and stuck it in the side of Doyle's neck. Doyle's eyes widened and watered, his arms flailing. Lyle pulled the knife out and watched as the bright arterial blood spurted from the confused young man. Lyle watched closely, with sadistic interest, as the life drained from Doyle's eyes. Doyle didn't understand why this was happening to him. He fought to stay alive. He pushed against Lyle, but he no longer had the strength. He kept on fighting until he couldn't anymore.

Greene and Lipton ran back through the tunnels and re-entered the club. Cartwright was sitting on the floor in the main room with a paramedic attending to his head wound. An officer was asking him questions. They went outside into the rain and saw McGovern standing by his car. Blinding lights were flashing all around them.

Greene walked up to McGovern. "Sir," she said, out of breath.

"What the hell happened here, Detective?" he shouted.

"We tried to take him in, as you said. It all went wrong."

"Yeah, I gathered that." He looked at Lipton who was leaning on the wall trying to regain his composure. He looked back at Greene. "Where is he?"

"He went out the back. There's an underground tunnel leading down the docks. He barricaded the door and we had to come back. His bodyguard shot at us. He's dead."

"Alright… we can handle it here, go find him."

"Yes sir."

She walked over to Lipton who was still trying to regain his breath, and gestured to him to follow. They went around the club and made their way down to the docks. They walked down the alley at the edge of the club. There were warehouses ahead and to the left and right of them. The port was massive. They stopped to figure out where Lyle would've gone.

Greene walked ahead of Lipton.

Lipton heard a muffled noise coming from amongst a pile of bins and discarded cardboard that sat beside the wall. He looked closer and saw Doyle lying amidst the trash heap.

"Fucking hell, Doyle!" He rushed over to him and held him by the head. "Greene!" he yelled.

She ran over to him and saw Doyle lying there in a pool of his own blood. He was still breathing, but only barely. "Officer down, back of the club, officer down," she yelled into her radio. She knelt by his side. "Where did he go?" she asked.

He didn't answer.

"Greene, you go," Lipton said. "Go find him, I'll stay with Doyle."

"Okay," she said. She was reluctant to leave them but she knew she couldn't do anything more to help.

The lamplights that lined the port became fewer the further she went. She made it to the end of the dock. At the end, some stairs led down to the sewer system. She looked down and saw the door that led to the tunnels. It was still barricaded shut.

In the distance - behind the ever-thickening curtain of rain - a boat light flickered. It was faint and Greene watched as it slowly faded out into the sea.

When she returned to where she had left Lipton and Doyle she found Lipton sitting on the wet concrete. He looked defeated. The two paramedics behind him were covering Doyle's head with a sheet. They stood on either side of the gurney that he lay on and they picked him up and carried him away.

Greene stood motionless and watched Doyle be taken away. She could feel her heart beat faster and harder. Her breath became short and violent. She rested against the wall and closed her eyes and held her chest. She tried to control her panic with the techniques she had learnt over the years. Nothing worked.

"I'm sorry," Lipton said quietly, looking at her.

"Don't be, it's not your fault, it's nobody's fault," Greene said. She felt her phone vibrate in her pocket. She ignored it.

"Still…" Lipton stood up and tried to wipe the water from the back of his trousers before he realised it was raining and it would be pointless.

"I know."

McGovern walked over looking angrier than before. "You two have done enough here, go home," he said. He didn't say anything more, he just looked down at the spot where Doyle had died then he shook his head and walked away.

Greene's phone rang again. "Shit," she said, giving a little chuckle. "I had dinner plans."

"You should go, I can deal with all of this."

"Are you sure?"

"Yeah, just go."

Greene left him and returned to her car. She got in and immediately started to cry. She tried to stop but couldn't. She held her head and leaned down so that nobody would see her. She let it all out, releasing all the emotion that had been building up inside her the last few days. It was cathartic. She regained control of herself a moment later and turned on the engine and backed out of the parking lot. While on the highway heading back to town, Len called her. She answered and put him on speaker.

"Hey," she said.

"I just heard about what happened, are you okay?"

"I'm okay, maybe a bit shaken up."

"I'm at the station now, but I'm heading over there. McGovern called and said he needed me there ASAP. Sorry about missing dinner."

"That's okay," she said, masking her sadness.

"I'll call you when I'm done, okay?"

"Okay. Thanks, Len."

"Talk later."

"Yeah, bye."

She hung up and wiped a single tear from her cheek.

❖ ❖ ❖

She sat in her car, watching Paul's house. The lights were on and she could see shadows pass by from behind the shades. She didn't want to socialise but she didn't want to give Paul the impression that she was regressing again. She looked at herself in the rearview mirror, her mascara had run down her cheeks. She took out a tissue and wiped it off. She took her time going up the steps to the door. She stood on the porch for a moment; The rain came down on her like a barrage. When she finally got the courage to ring the doorbell, she felt an awful sinking feeling in her stomach.

Paul opened the door and smiled at her. "I'm so glad you made it," he said cheerfully.

"Thanks for inviting me," she said, clearing her throat halfway through.

"Come in, please. The weather's turned quick," he said, looking up at the black sky.

As she stepped inside Alex ran up to her and hugged her tightly around the legs. Greene looked down at her and suddenly felt all her sadness and anxiety pass.

"Hi, sweetie! Did you have a good day," Greene said, brushing her daughter's hair behind her ear.

Alex didn't respond, she just hugged her tighter.

"Dinner's almost ready," Paul said. He walked past Greene and Alex and walked towards the kitchen. "I didn't think you were going to make it. We were about to start without you."

Greene didn't say anything, she thought he was making a dig at her.

"Oh, by the way, Meredith," Paul said. He came back to the entranceway where Alex remained with her mother in a vice. "This is Josephine."

Greene looked up at Paul standing next to a nice, simple-looking woman. She was about the same age as her but with dark hair, and a more petite frame.

"It's so nice to finally meet you," Josephine said. "Paul and Alex have told me so much, I've been looking forward to meeting you for a while."

"It's nice to meet you too," Greene said. She looked down at Alex. "You're going to have to let go of me sometime. How are we going to eat?"

Alex let go of her and ran into the kitchen and stood on her tiptoes and leaned over the stove to smell what was cooking.

Greene followed all three of them to the dining table. "Smells delicious," she said.

"Thanks! I've cooked us a lobster and I've got a clam chowder on the stove," Josephine said.

"Jo loves seafood," Paul said, shaking his head jokingly. "I'm not sick of it... yet."

"Hey now!" exclaimed Josephine, hitting him lovingly on the arm. She turned off the stove and moved the pot with the chowder onto a wooden placemat in the centre of the dining table. The lobster was already prepared on the table.

"Please sit, want something to drink?" Paul said.

"I wouldn't say no to a beer if you've got one?" Greene said. She sat down and Alex sat beside her. Bowls and utensils were already in front of them. They looked at each other and smiled and made funny faces at one another.

Paul handed Greene a beer and sat down.

Josephine poured the clam chowder into all four bowls. "Help yourself to the lobster and the bread. Have at it!" she said.

Thunder clapped and roared outside.

"Woah, thunder!" Alex said, looking up at her mother with excitement.

"It's going to be a big storm, they say," Josephine added. "It's supposed to last the rest of the week."

"Maybe they will cancel school," Alex said.

"Don't bet on it," Paul said, chuckling.

"So, Meredith…" Josephine said while dunking a chunk of lobster meat into her bowl of chowder. "I understand you're a detective, what's that like?"

Suddenly the events of the day came back to the forefront of Greene's mind and she felt her anxiety returning. "Uh, yeah. It's okay, there's not much crime around here."

"That's lucky."

"And you work with Paul at the school, right?" Greene asked, changing the subject.

"Right! I teach first grade."

"Oh right, I forgot that you're Alex's teacher."

"That's okay. You should come to the next parent-teacher meeting."

"Uh, that's more Paul's thing, I don't do that—"

"That's alright, I don't judge," Josephine said innocently.

"Why would you judge me?"

"Oh, no. I didn't mean—"

"What did you mean? You don't know me."

"Meredith, please?" Paul said.

"I'm sorry," Josephine said. She was getting visibly upset. "I really didn't mean anything by that, I'm sorry."

"No, I'm sorry," Greene said, feeling embarrassed. "I get defensive sometimes, I'm sorry."

"Let's just have a nice dinner, please?" Paul said.

They all went quiet and returned to their meal.

Paul reached over the table and held Josephine's hand. "Jo's a great teacher, she genuinely cares about the children," he said.

"I'd hope so," Greene said with snark.

"I've always loved working with children," Josephine said, "I grew up with three younger siblings and I was always the one who'd have to babysit and care for them, but I didn't mind, I actually really loved doing it. So naturally I had to go into teaching—"

"Naturally."

"—I uh, just fell in love with it, and with this town. It's all so wonderful." She looked at Paul lovingly, "I couldn't be happier."

"Well, that's good. I'm happy for the both of you," Greene said, in an attempt to be polite.

"Thank you," Paul and Josephine said together.

Greene finished her bowl of chowder and felt a bit warm and took off her jacket. She leaned back in her chair with her hands resting on her belly.

"Meredith, you're bleeding!" Paul said.

Greene looked down at herself and saw that her left shirt sleeve had turned red. "Oh!" she said calmly. She lifted her sleeve and saw the small gash across her shoulder.

"I'll get the first aid kit," Josephine said. She jumped out of her chair and rushed out of the kitchen and headed upstairs.

Paul got up and knelt down beside her. "Jesus Christ, Meredith. What happened?" he said with great concern.

"I didn't even notice," she said. "We got into a little shootout earlier, guess I got hit."

"A little shootout? What the fuck?"

Alex looked over at her mom and at her bloody arm. Her little eyes welled up, and she began to wail.

"It's alright hun, it's just a scratch. Mommy will be fine," Greene said.

Josephine came back down the stairs in such a rush that she cleared the bottom three steps. She ran into the kitchen and handed the first aid kit to Paul. He opened it and took out the bandages, as well as the bottle of peroxide and the needle and thread.

Greene unbuttoned her shirt and lowered it below her shoulder. The gash was two inches long and half an inch wide. It looked quite deep.

"Don't worry, we're required to do first aid training for school," Josephine said.

Paul put some peroxide on a clean cloth and wiped her wound clean. It stung terribly but Greene didn't let it be known. The bleeding must have ceased over an hour ago because it had coagulated and took a few firm wipes to get it clean. He then threaded the needle with the black thread and carefully stitched up the wound.

Greene continued to brave the pain. She smiled through it all and even made funny faces to Alex to reassure her that everything was alright. Alex eventually stopped crying.

Paul bandaged her up. He made sure he was gentle. "All done," he said.

"Thanks, Paul."

"You're welcome!" he said, putting the remaining bandages and thread back into the kit.

There was a knock at the door.

"I'll get it," Josephine said, rushing out of the kitchen. She opened the front door and saw Len standing there, drenched, holding his coat over his head.

"Hi, uh, I'm Len. I'm not sure I've got the right place?" he said.

"Who is it?" Paul yelled from the kitchen.

"Paul, is that you?" Len yelled back.

"Len?" Paul said, peeking out into the hall. "Come on in, you must be freezing."

Josephine opened the door wide and Len quickly stepped inside out of the cold rain.

"Let me get your coat," she said.

"Oh, thank you!" Len said. He took off his coat, dripping wet, and handed it to her and she hung it on the coat rack by the door.

"I'm Josephine, by the way."

"Len, nice to meet you!" he replied. They shook hands and then went into the dining room. Len saw Greene sitting there, her shirt lowered down to her chest and the bandage around her arm. "Oh god, what happened?"

"It seems I got shot," Greene said.

"Are you okay, do we need to go to the clinic?" Len said. He knelt beside her.

"I'm fine, it's only a scratch."

"I've stitched it up and bandaged it. Should heal just fine," Paul said,

"Yeah, don't worry about me," she said with a smile.

"That's a relief," Len said. He softly grabbed her hand and held it between his.

"There's plenty of food left over if you're hungry," Josephine said.

"Oh yes! Please. I'm starving."

"I'll get you a bowl."

"Thank you."

Paul grabbed Len a chair and sat him next to Greene. Josephine filled a bowl with chowder and placed it in front of him.

"Enjoy!" she said.

"Thank you very much."

Alex tugged at Len's damp shirt. "Hi!" she said.

"Hi!" he said back. "You must be Alex."

She giggled and turned shyly away from him.

Josephine sat back down. "So, Len…" she said, "how long have you and Meredith been seeing each other?"

"Oh?" He looked at Greene, shrugged, then turned back. "About two days?"

"Wow," she laughed. "Okay. So, this *is* new?"

"Just a bit," he said, chewing on a clam.

The night continued. It was a pleasant dinner for all involved. Alex went to bed not long after, and the four of them sat in the living room and talked about everything and nothing. By the night's end, Greene and Josephine were laughing together and small-talking as if they were old friends. Paul took Len out to the garage to show him his motorcycle - An old 1964 Triumph Bonneville - which he had been renovating for the past two years. Jo and Greene shared a bottle of red and talked about life and love and what brought them joy.

It was 10pm when Greene and Len left. They said their goodbyes and Greene hugged Paul and Josephine. The weather had continued to get worse. The downpour was significant, the gutters were filled and overflowing onto the streets.

"You okay to drive?" Len asked Greene.

"Probably not," she replied, cackling. She wasn't drunk by any means, she'd only had a couple, but the thought of driving in this weather caused her to worry.

"I'll drive, we'll take my car," he said.

They got into Len's car and he drove her home. On the way, she thought all about what had happened that night. Getting shot at wasn't something she ever thought would happen to her. It's not like it was something she thought couldn't happen, she wasn't oblivious to the risks of the job. But the reality of almost getting killed felt foreign. He parked outside her apartment. She got out and leaned in through the passenger window.

"Want to come in? I could use the company," she asked.

"Okay, I'll come in, but if you think I'm going to sleep with you, you've got the wrong end of the stick."

"That so?"

"That's right, I'm a good catholic boy," he said, grinning widely.

"Shut up and get inside."

They ran from the street, up the stairs to her apartment. The rain bombarded them. Just the short distance from the street was enough to soak them both. They stood outside her door. Greene unlocked her door and they quickly stepped inside. They were out of breath, and laughed.

"Shh," she said, stumbling inside. "Mrs. Driscoll next door will be furious if we woke her."

She threw her keys onto the kitchen counter as she entered her apartment and they both took off their coats and hung them up. Len shut the door behind him and then he looked around her home. Curious how his other half lived. It was only a small studio apartment, but he was impressed by it. They stood by the kitchen, drenched from head to toe. They looked at each other with lust. Her black bra was visible through her wet, white shirt. He moved close to her, close enough to wrap his arm around her waist. He pressed his pelvis into hers and lifted her up and placed her on the kitchen counter. They kissed passionately and he unbuttoned her shirt and pulled it off over her shoulders and as he did so he brushed against her bandaged arm and she let out a cry.

"Shit, sorry," he said. He moved away from her slightly. "Are you okay?"

She grabbed her arm and held it. She grimaced. "Yeah, I'm fine. It just stings a little."

A trickle of blood seeped through the bandage.

"Damn, I think I pulled a stitch," he said.

Greene laughed a little. "How rude," she said jokingly. "It'll be okay. I'll just get my kit from the bathroom." She hopped off the counter and walked to the bathroom then returned with a small first aid kit. She sat down on the sofa and he sat beside her and he helped her remove the bandage. A stitch had torn out through her skin. Len got the scissors from the kit and cut the torn stitching loose, then restitched it. He was careful not to hurt her. He bandaged her back up.

"There," he said, taping the bandage.

"Thanks," she said.

"What happened at the club?" he asked.

"Ah, it all went to shit. We went to bring in Lyle Pentaghast. Well, we tried anyway. He ran. His bodyguard - or whomever he was - shot at us and we were forced to fire back. I didn't even know I'd been hit until I took my jacket off at dinner. It's strange how something doesn't hurt you until you realize it exists."

"What happened to the guy who shot at you?"

"We shot him. He's dead."

"Oh."

"Yeah. It was the first time I've ever had to shoot someone. And the first time I've ever been shot at. Surprising, I know! I've been doing this for fifteen years… I guess my luck ran out. I just don't know how to feel about it, or how I'm supposed to feel."

"You had to defend yourself," he said, putting his arm around her.

"Of course, I know that. I don't think I regret it, I just wish I didn't have to do it in the first place."

"I'm sorry."

"It's okay."

She rested her head on his shoulder and placed her right arm over his chest. The two of them laid back on the sofa, their arms tightly wound around each other.

◆ ◆ ◆

"What an awful fucking day," Captain McGovern said, looking through the observation window of the morgue at the body of Officer Doyle lying on a slab. He turned to Lipton who was standing next to him. "How did it come to this?"

"It just… went wrong."

"Went wrong? A man's dead. He's married, you know? Got a kid on the way. Is that what I should tell her? That it went wrong?"

"I didn't know he had a family," he said, bowing his head.

"Can you at least tell me where Lyle Pentaghast is? Do you have any fucking idea?"

"No."

McGovern shook his head. "Christ, Daniel."

"I know."

"In the morning I need you and Greene to give a full account of the day, clear?"

"Clear."

"Good. Now go on home and get some sleep, you look awful."

Lipton left the morgue. He felt as if he'd been hit by a truck. His head throbbed, and his stomach ached. He got into his car and let out a brief yell and smacked the steering wheel with the palm of his hand. He pulled out of the station. It was dark and the storm had reached the town in force. Thunder roared overhead and the night sky lit up intermittently with lightning. He began his drive heading home but changed his mind halfway there, and turned back round and headed back towards the port.

The parking lot of Misty's was still cordoned off and two officers were standing guard outside the entrance. Lipton parked and got out and greeted the officers with a smile and a wave. He told them he was just following up on a few things and he wanted to take a look around. They didn't object, and let him through. He went inside the empty club. The lights were still on and when he walked through he felt a bizarre sensation, a sort of chill, like he was walking through a graveyard at night. He went up the stairs at the back and walked down the hall past the empty changing rooms to Cartwright's office. He didn't knock. He thrust the door open and charged in.

"No!" Cartwright yelled, standing out of his chair. His neck bruised, and his jaw swollen.

Lipton went around the desk and grabbed him and threw him over it. He landed hard on the floor. Cartwright rolled around in pain and held his head. Lipton came back around and picked him back up and pinned him against his desk.

"What do you want? I told the cops everything," Cartwright said.

"I want you to listen to me," Lipton said with a tranquil tone.

"Yeah, ok."

"I don't really care what you've done, I don't care about you at all. What I want is the Pentaghasts. I know you transport girls to them—"

"I don't know what you're—"

"Shut the fuck up and listen… just listen. This Friday, just like every Friday before, you're going to do just that. You're going to take the girls by van to wherever they need to go—"

"They won't do it," Cartwright said, wheezing throughout. "They're not stupid, they know you're onto them. They won't risk it."

"Then you make them risk it. Tell them whatever you need to. Tell them you have new girls that they'd hate to miss out on, understood? Because it's in your best interest to make this happen because if you don't I'm going to come back and I'm going to break your fucking skull!"

"Alright, alright. You don't have to threaten me. I'll do it. I'm on your side. He tried to kill me, remember?"

"Good, and make sure you use a burner. They're listening," Lipton said. He released the trembling Cartwright from his vice and walked out of the office and didn't look back.

❖ ❖ ❖

Albert Pentaghast was sitting in his chair. The warm fire roaring in front of him. He had a lit cigar in one hand, and he was fidgeting with an antique gold coin in the other. The gold sheen had faded, but the swastika was as clear as the day it was minted.

His butler came into the room holding a phone. "A call for you, sir. It's Lyle," he said.

Albert gestured to him to hand him the phone. He put it up to his ear. "What is it?" he said.

Lyle was on his boat, a small speedboat that they often used for fishing, among other things. He was moored at a small isolated dock hidden amidst the islets a few miles up the coast from town.

"Something happened. I made a mistake," Lyle said, barely able to get the words out.

There was no answer.

"Did you hear me?" he repeated.

"I heard you. Tell me what happened?" Albert said.

"I went to Misty's to speak with Errol, as you suggested, and the cops showed and… fuck."

"Spit it out."

"Virgil's dead. I got out but some cop got in my way and—"

"You killed him?"

"Yes."

"And they can identify you?"

"I don't know, maybe. I think so."

"Where are you now?"

"At the wharf by the cabin."

"Good, stay there for now. And don't call here again."

Albert hung up the phone and handed it back to the butler. "Stupid boy," he said.

Lyle walked up from the wharf to the cabin with the rain hitting his back. It was a small fishing hut by the shore. The wood it was made of was beginning to rot and there was the persistent smell of dead fish in the air. He stepped inside and grabbed a log and some newspaper from beside the stone fireplace and threw it on. He lit it with his gold-plated lighter that he received from his father for his twenty-fifth birthday. The wind howled and thrashed against the windows, and the outside shutters flew back and forth striking the glass. He looked back at the far corner of the cabin. Dark and shadowed. A blood-stained chair bolted to the ground. Rope coiled around the base of its legs. A soiled mattress in the corner.

He grinned, then sat in front of the fire and warmed his hands. The wind died down but the rain continued to get progressively heavier as the night went on.

His phone rang. He thought it might have been his father. "Yes?" he said.

"It's Errol," said the voice on the other end.

"Fucking hell, Errol, you're still alive? What are you calling me for?"

Errol was sitting at his desk, nursing the back of his neck. "That detective came to my office twenty minutes ago."

"The woman?"

"No, the other one. The one with the big head."

"And?"

"He wanted me to organise another event with you, up at the lodge. He said he would follow us and catch you, or something along those lines. I couldn't hear every word with his hands around my neck."

Lyle lowered the phone to his waist and went deep into thought. He watched a spider crawl up the wall.

"Uh, you still there?" Cartwright asked.

"Yeah, I'm still here. I think it's a great idea, let's do it!"

"What? What do you mean? I called you to warn you about him."

"That piece of shit killed Virgil. You call him back and tell him that it's all a go for Friday night. He'll follow you to the lodge and I'll be there waiting for him."

"It's dangerous. He gave me the impression that he wants to kill you. What if that's his plan?"

"That's good, don't you see? He's unhinged, unpredictable, thinks he's above the law. Nobody will know about it, and nobody will care or be surprised when he disappears. Don't worry about it, Errol. I'm going to kill him first."

V

There was a sudden loud knock at the door. Greene was woken up and felt Len's heartbeat through his chest. She looked up at his waking expression. He looked down at her, and they smiled. There was another knock. Len looked to the door and said he would get it. He got up off the sofa and did a little run over to the door. He peered through the peephole.

"It's Lipton," Len said, looking back at her.

She nodded and made an inward waving gesture. He opened the door and Lipton came in without hesitation. He looked at Len then at Greene who was sitting upright on the sofa.

"Good, you're both here. I've got a plan," he said. He sat down on one of the kitchen barstools.

"What's the time?" Greene said, still half asleep.

"Six-thirty," Lipton said, looking at his watch. "I know it's early, but I had to talk to you."

Len sat back down on the sofa and the two of them looked at Lipton with bated breath, waiting for him to impart something important.

"I received a call from Errol Cartwright late last night—"

"You what?" Greene said.

"Yeah. I went to the club last night and I had a good talk with him and convinced him to help us get to Lyle. He's organized one of his parties for tomorrow night. We're going to follow them to the event and catch them in the act."

"That's insane!" Len said.

"Yeah, you're probably right. But I feel it's our best - and likely the only - chance we'll have. We know Lyle will be at the event, and I doubt we'd be able to find him otherwise."

"What does Captain McGovern say?"

"I haven't told him anything. He won't allow this. We haven't got the manpower to do a raid by tomorrow and by the time it takes to get the state police on board he'll be long gone. This is our one opportunity to get the bastard."

"I'm in," Greene said.

"You've got to be kidding?" Len said. He stood up. "You have to let the captain know about this."

"Look, Leonard, I'm doing this with or without your help," Lipton said.

Len shook his head. He looked down at Greene. "Are you seriously going to go along with this?"

She looked up at him. "Ever since the beginning of this investigation, we all knew it would end like this, at one of those parties. If Daniel says it's the only way to catch Lyle, then I believe him. I'm in."

"Jesus Christ," Len said, flapping his arms in defeat. "Goddamn it, fine. I can't let you both do it alone. I guess you can count me it."

"Good, I've set up a meeting with Cartwright tonight at Seven. We'll meet him out the back of his club." He hopped off the barstool and headed to the door then looked back at Greene. "I'll meet you there?"

"Okay," she said.

Lipton nodded and relaxed his shoulders. "Good, and thank you," he said. He opened the door and left the apartment.

Len closed the door behind him and then looked back at her. "Seriously? This is insane!" he said.

"I know it is!" she said, with a measure of uncertainty. "But you haven't seen what Lipton has in his basement. The walls are covered in evidence linking the Pentaghasts to murders going back to the early eighties. We have to stop them, and I trust Lipton. He knows what he's doing."

"Does he? How long have we known him? Four days?"

"Long enough."

◆ ◆ ◆

McGovern ordered everybody to the briefing room. He stood in front of the evidence-covered boards waiting patiently for everyone to sit. He watched them all find their seats.

"Everyone's here? Good," he said. "First off, at four o'clock this afternoon, there will be a memorial service for Officer Matthew Doyle at the Colossal Squid, I expect you all to attend. His funeral will be beforehand, but it's only going to be a small family affair. We will also be taking a collection, for his family. But until then, we need to find Lyle Pentaghast." He pointed to a DMV photo of him on the board. "He is our main priority. Not only is he wanted for the murder of Officer Doyle but he is also our main suspect in the murder of Jessica Perdeaux. Greene's the lead on the case. Any leads?"

Greene was so distracted by the thought of tomorrow's plan that she didn't hear him calling her name.

"Greene!" he yelled.

"Yes sir?" she said, breaking free of her trance.

"Any leads on our suspect?"

"No sir, he's in the wind. We've got an APB out on him with the state police and local sheriffs, as well as the coastguard."

"Good, he shouldn't be able to allude us for long. What about his family? Connections?"

"His father, Albert Pentaghast lives about two hours north. And he's got no other family that we know of. We know he's connected to Errol Cartwright, but we don't know how well."

"We questioned Cartwright for three hours last night and he didn't tell us squat. He said that Pentaghast was just a VIP client, that's all. We have no evidence to the contrary so we had to let him go. I guess we'll just have to wait until Lyle shows up. He has to show up sometime." He waved them away and sighed. "Back to work!" he said.

Lipton and Greene stood alone in the briefing room, looking at the evidence on display. Greene turned to him. "We should tell the Captain," she said.

"He won't agree to it. He'll only get in the way."

"Okay… if you're sure?"

"I am."

There was silence.

◆ ◆ ◆

Doctor Wallis didn't say anything. She sat calmly and watched Greene from across the room. She lightly tapped her pen against her notebook. The rain had started falling again as it had been on and off since last night. It was loud and struck the windows with great force.

"The weather's strange," Doctor Wallis said. "For summer, I mean. We don't usually get this type of storm this time of the year."

"No, I suppose we don't," Greene said.

"I heard on the news about an officer that was killed on duty last night. How are you doing?"

"I'm fine. We were involved in a shooting with two suspects and one of the suspects got away. He killed Doyle while fleeing. It was... pretty horrible, but I'm fine now."

"Alright. Did you know the officer well?"

"No, not really. He hadn't been at the job for very long, but he seemed nice. He has a wife. Never met her. I think she's pregnant."

"A sad thing. It must be hard to lose a colleague on the job—"

"It's not something that happens here, so it's a shock for sure. But I've never let things like that worry me before and I'm not going to now. If I was worried about dying on the job every day, I'd have become a lawyer."

"You finished law school, right?"

"Yeah, passed the bar and everything. My father was a prosecutor and my mother was a nurse so I suppose I was always destined to become a public servant. He was very upset when I joined the police. He said I'd end up getting myself killed. Maybe I will, who knows. But this is what I wanted to do and I'll continue to do it until I can't anymore."

She looked out the window but saw nothing but rain.

"Do you mind if we change the subject?" Greene asked.

"Of course. What would you like to talk about?"

"Nothing."

"Okay, that's perfectly fine."

They sat in silence for a while. The clock on the wall ticked in the background, slowly stealing away the hour. The rain temporarily ceased outside and a short ray of sunshine shone through the west-facing windows then the rain came back again.

"How's your relationship with Len?" Wallis asked.

"Oh, good. I think. We went to the movie theatre Tuesday night."

"What did you see?"

"Uh," she had to think about it, "The Umbrellas Of Cherbourg. Yeah, that was it. Have you seen it?"

"Oh yes. Jacques Demy. Catherine Deneuve. It's a personal favorite of mine. My father took me to the theatre to see it when I was a child, back in, oh, I don't know how long ago now. Did you like the film?"

"It was good, I think I liked the experience more than anything. Just being on a date with someone made me forget about everything… for a while anyway. Last night we had dinner with Paul and his new girlfriend."

"How did that go?"

"Good, I think. I finally met Josephine - that's the new girlfriend - she was nice. I think I was a bit rude at one point. It wasn't intentional. Paul seems happy with her so I think it's good for everyone, including Alex. They both seem to really like each other."

"You're both moving on."

"He is. I'm trying to. Len took me home last night, we didn't have sex, we just sat together on the sofa until we fell asleep. I'm not sure what that means."

"It means that you feel safe with him."

"Yeah, maybe." She considered that for a moment. "I think you might be right."

"It's a good thing, Meredith. It's progress. Two years ago you wouldn't have even considered a relationship let alone allowing someone new to get close to you. This is good."

"Yeah," Greene smiled. "It is good."

◆ ◆ ◆

Greene arrived at The Colossal Squid at four o'clock on the chime. She once again wore her only suit, and this time she was grateful for its blandness. She entered the pub and saw her colleagues gathered in the back, all chatting and reminiscing. Roland was standing behind the bar, pouring pints of ale and placing them on a tray. He saw Greene standing in the doorway.

"Ahoy there, Greene!" he called out. He waved her over.

"Good afternoon, Roland," she said, approaching the bar.

"Sad occasion, can I get you a drink?"

"Just a beer, please."

"Of course, coming right up." He grabbed a freshly washed glass from below the bar and filled it with ale from the tap. "Here ye go," he said, handing it to her.

"Thanks, Roland. I'm going to go join them," she said. He waved at her as she walked over to the others. A couple of officers were playing pool and some others were consoling Doyle's widow. The widow was young, barely of drinking age, dressed in black, and had her hands resting on her bulging belly. She was weeping, and telling everybody who would listen how excited they were to become parents.

Len walked up to Greene and gave her a light kiss on the cheek and a comforting hug. "Hey!" he said.

"Hey you!" she said with a smile.

They didn't say anything more, they just stood next to each other, showing support by being present at the solemn occasion.

McGovern stood in front of everyone. He stepped up onto a crate and clinked his glass with a spoon. "Alright! Alright!" he said, grabbing the attention of everyone in the room. "I'd like to thank you all for coming. We're here to mourn our colleague and friend, Matthew Doyle. But we're also here to celebrate his life. He was one of the finest young officers I've ever had the honor of working with. He had conviction, and he took great pride in his work. He was loved and respected by all who knew him, and we'll miss him dearly. I want to make a toast to him. Please, everybody, raise your glasses to Matthew. To Matthew, the best of us!"

"To Matthew, the best of us!" everybody said together with their glasses raised.

"And to Jenny," he said to the widow. "I want you to know that you'll always be a part of this family. We're all going to be there for you and your child. If you need anything, we'll be there."

The widow smiled bitterly through her tears.

A couple of hours passed and the wake was all but ended.

"It's almost time to go," Lipton said, joining Greene and Len at the bar.

"Yeah," she said without looking at him. "It was a nice service."

Lipton looked around the pub. Half the guests had already gone home and the widow was getting ready to leave, she was putting on her coat by the door. He finished his small glass of scotch and pushed it across the bar.

"Come on, best to get there early," he said.

"Alright," Greene said, taking one last sip of her beer. She turned around on the barstool and hopped off it.

"Be careful. Call me after?" Len said.

She looked back at him, nodded, and patted him on the thigh. She followed Lipton out of the pub. The rain was coming down strong and the wind blew her hair uncontrollably. All day the weather had come and gone in furious uncertainty, never knowing whether to stay or go. They went to his car and got in. He turned on the radio and Pat Mallory was beginning the six-thirty newscast.

"Ho boy the weather continues to pummel us, doesn't it folks? Our experts say it's not expected to clear until Saturday so strap in for a wild couple of days. I've been told by the coastguard to issue a warning to not go into the water at this time due to the increased chances of riptides and large waves. Just be safe out there, folks. Now onto some sad news. I'm sorry to report the death of one of our finest boys in blue. Matthew Doyle, died last night aged 26. He was killed while making an arrest in connection to the murder of Jessica Perdeaux. Gosh, what a tragedy. I'm told the suspect got away, what a calamity. It's been four days since the investigation into the young woman's death began and nobody's yet to be arrested. I don't know about you folks, but I'm starting to get worried that nobody's going to get done for this heinous crime. What are they doing out there? The man or men responsible are still out there. What if they kill again? Let's all pray to God that our fine officers in blue can keep us all safe—"

"Is he the only radio host you have in this town, Jesus Christ, what a tool," Lipton said before turning off the radio.

"Hey now!" Greene said, slapping him lightly on the shoulder. "That's our one and only local celebrity you're insulting there."

"Sorry, but you all could do a lot better."

"Okay, he's a bit of an asshole, I'll admit to that."

"Just a bit?"

Lipton pulled out onto the street and they headed for Misty's once again.

◆ ◆ ◆

The night had come early tonight, the black rainclouds blocked out all of the remaining light from the sun. Despite the horrid weather, the town didn't change. They passed people out to dinner with their families, and they saw prostitutes standing under whatever cover they could find while still keeping themselves visible to their prospective clientele. The gradual shift in class became more clear to Lipton the more times they drove back and forth from town to the port. The town's devolution from the quaint, beautiful haven that he loved into a ramshackle hovel became clear to him the more times he travelled the roads. The trailer parks and the unkempt homes belonging to the dregs of society revealed themselves to him. The painting of paradise that he'd created in his head had dissipated and the reality had finally sunk in.

They drove around the back of the club, driving down the seemingly never-ending alley that stretched from the highway to the ocean. It was quiet. Nobody was around, and the only sounds were those of the rain, wind, and waves crashing against the wharves. Seagulls squawked around them, sitting on the gutters of the abandoned warehouses and boatsheds. They parked, and sat in the car, waiting.

"Is this where we're meeting him?" Greene asked.

"Yeah, this is it." Lipton checked his watch to make sure he wasn't too late or too early. "He should be here by now," he said.

Out of the warehouse in front of them, a beam of light shone out of the open doors. The detectives squinted and shielded their eyes. The light dimmed and they saw Cartwright standing in the doorway waving to them.

"Here we go," Lipton said.

They both exited the car, and were instantly bombarded by the rain. They ran over to the warehouse and quickly got under cover. Cartwright shut the doors behind them and stood waiting.

"We're here, what do you have to tell us?" Lipton asked.

Cartwright walked over to a wooden stool in the corner of the large, empty room. He sat down and lit himself a cigarette.

"Well?" Lipton repeated.

Cartwright took a long drag and then spat tobacco onto the floor. "It's all on for tomorrow, as you said."

"That's good."

"There's a few problems."

"Like what?"

"Well, he knows."

"He knows?"

"Yeah, he knows. Hear me out, okay? I told 'im what you wanted me to do —"

"You fuck!" Lipton yelled.

"Listen! I thought it was the only way to get 'im to agree to it. He tried to kill me, remember? He would've known it was a trap anyway so by me telling 'im the truth, he now trusts me. You see? Reverse psychology. He knows you're coming so he believes he's got the upper hand. But he doesn't know that you know that he knows… you know?"

Lipton groaned.

"I think this might work," Greene said.

"It won't work though," Cartwright said as he took another drag.

"What do you mean?" Greene said, taking a step closer.

"So, okay, you want to follow us up to the lodge, fine, you can do that. But you won't get in. The whole area's fenced off. And there will be a lot of security. These people don't fuck about, and the two of you won't be able to pull it off… no offense."

"Why the fuck are we here then?" Lipton said.

"I 'ave a better idea, it'll be dangerous though."

"We're listening," Greene said.

"You," he said, pointing to Greene, "you'll be able to get in—"

"How so?" she asked.

"You go in as one of the girls—"

"Woah, fuck no!" Lipton said.

"It's the only way you'll get in, and once you're in you can find a way to get the big man in too. There's a side gate in the fence that you can get to by following a path through the woods. Open that and the two of you can get on with doing whatever the fuck you're planning to do."

Greene didn't say anything, she bowed her head in thought.

"This is madness," Lipton said.

Cartwright turned to Lipton and shrugged. "It's up to you, but believe me, you ain't getting in any other way. When we're in I can help get her out of the lodge quietly so that she can get to the gate. It'll work."

"Okay," Greene said.

"What?" Lipton said, turning to her.

"I can do it!" she said confidently, "don't argue with me, I'm doing this."

"If you're sure?"

"I'm sure."

"Great!" Cartwright blurted. "We'll need to get you a whole getup. A dress, shoes, some jewelery. Make sure you look the part. I've got some spares in the club. Shall we take a look?"

"Alright, lead the way," she said.

Cartwright jumped from his seat and headed for the door, and Greene began to follow. Lipton grabbed her arm and held her back.

"This is a fucking bad idea, Greene," Lipton said. "You could be killed, or worse. I don't want to be responsible for you being hurt."

"You won't be," she said, peeling his hand from her arm. "I can handle myself."

She followed Cartwright out of the warehouse.

"Goddamned mad... all of you," Lipton said.

They followed Cartwright out of the warehouse and down the alley to the club's back entrance. They turned left as they entered and followed the hall around to the main floor. They went up the stairs to the changing rooms. In the rooms were vanities covered in makeup kits and loose lingerie. Cartwright opened a large wardrobe - that stretched the length of the room - that was filled with a variety of dresses and costumes.

"Take your pick," he said.

"I don't think any of these will fit me," she said, searching through the wardrobe.

"Sure they will, what are you, a ten?"

"Thereabouts."

"Right," he said. He went to the other side of the wardrobe and searched through the dresses, taking a quick look at each one. "Aha!" He pulled out a long blue satin dress. It was beautiful. Something you'd see a starlet wear.

Lipton stood in the doorway, quiet, shaking his head disapprovingly.

"This will work," Cartwright said. He held the dress up to her and nodded. He handed it to her.

She held it up in front of herself and looked in the mirror. It looked perfect, almost like it was made for her.

"Be here tomorrow night at six, alright? Make sure you come in the back way. I'll 'ave one of my girls help you into the dress and get you looking right." He clapped his hands. "So... we good?"

"Yeah," she said, handing him back the dress. "We're good."

"Good, now kindly fuck off! I'd rather you two not be 'ere a second longer than you 'ave to."

They left and went back to their car. They sat for a moment, contemplating their decisions.

"You know Len won't go along with this," he said.

"I'll convince him."

"You can try, but I doubt he'll listen. He cares about you too much to let you go through with this."

❖ ❖ ❖

She called Len when she got home and asked him to come over. It was late - past ten - and the sound of the rain had become a permanent fixture in the soundscape of the town. He knocked on the door and she opened it for him and invited him in. She offered him a drink but he politely refused and sat himself down on the sofa.

"So what did he say?" he asked.

She didn't sit next to him, she instead sat on one of the barstools by her kitchen counter.

"It's on for tomorrow night," she said.

"Okay." He rubbed his face anxiously. "What's the plan?"

"Before I tell you, promise me that you'll listen to everything I say and not overreact?"

He squinted a little. "Alright, I promise."

"Tomorrow night at six o'clock I'm going to Misty's. There I'm going to get made up like the other girls and Cartwright is going to bring me into the party—"

"You what? No fucking way!" he said sharply.

"What did I just ask?"

"I-I'm sorry, but that's insane. It's too dangerous."

"I know it's a risk. But it's our best shot. He says the place we're going to is surrounded by a fence and there will be security and who knows what else. Cartwright said that there is a side gate far from the lodge that I'll be able to open from the inside and let Lipton in. And from there we can do what we need to."

"I don't like it."

"You don't have to. This is happening. I just need your support. Please?"

He bowed his head and scratched the back of his neck. "You have it, you know you have it," he said.

"Thank you, Len… truly."

"So, what's my role in this plan? I don't think I'd be much help in a fight —"

"You'll wait in the car."

"Excellent…"

"We'll need a quick way out, and if anything does go wrong we'll need you to call for backup."

"Great, absolutely great plan," he said, shaking his head.

She went over to him and sat next to him. She put her hand on his thigh and rested her head against his shoulder. He looked at her from the corner of his eye and placed his hand on hers and they sat in silence.

"I think I'll take that drink now," he said.

She chuckled, got up, and went over to the kitchen. She pulled out a bottle of merlot from the wine rack nestled in the cabinet high above the counter and poured two small glasses and walked over to the sofa where he sat and handed him a glass. She sat down next to him and they clanked their glasses together and laid back on the couch and drank their wine.

She put the wine glass down and took off the plain cardigan he wore, and draped it over the arm of the sofa. She looked at him longingly. He put his glass down and looked back at her with the same intention. They leaned in closer to each other. He held her cheeks softly and kissed her. She kissed him back. She shuffled ever closer to him and put her hand on his chest and caressed him. He did the same with her, he lowered his hand to her thigh and held her close. He stopped for a moment and held her cheek again.

"Are you sure?" he asked, with heavy breath.

"Yes! Definitely, yes!" she said.

He pushed her back on the couch and got down on his knees. She was surprised, but pleasantly so. He unbuttoned her trousers and gripped the waistband and he pulled them down onto the floor. He then kissed her thigh and reached up and slowly pulled down her underwear. He threw them onto the floor and his head disappeared between her legs. She felt him. She felt his passion. She leaned her head back and relaxed into it, feeling it all. She let herself get lost in the sensation. She grabbed his head and pushed him away from her, his face looked shocked until she leaned forward and kissed him, wrapping her arms around his neck. She stood him up and pushed him back onto the sofa, she unbuckled his belt and unzipped his trousers. She reciprocated. She felt him in her hand, and in her mouth.

He carried her to bed, just like a newlywed would. They took off all their remaining clothes and he lay on top of her and kissed her neck. Greene leaned over to her bedside cabinet and pulled out a condom and helped him put it on then she guided him inside her. The feelings she felt during were indescribable. The joy, the comfort, the pleasure. She held him tightly as he thrust. He caressed her waist, her ass, and her breasts with all possible enthusiasm and love. This was more than just two people fucking… this was real, passionate love. Two people lost in an intimate embrace. Both of them revelling in each other's pleasure.

She looked to her left, at Len lying beside her. Her thigh was resting against his penis. She quietly laughed. She could still taste him, and smell him. She placed her hand on her forehead and sighed happily. Len opened his eyes and rolled over onto his back and yawned. He looked at Greene and smiled at her.

"Hey," she said.

"What are you thinking?" he asked.

"Nothing," she said, shaking her head. "I'm just happy."

He moved over closer to her and kissed her. She grabbed his head and kissed him back. They just laid there for a while, holding one another, staring into each other's eyes, and smiling.

VI

The wind howled fiercely throughout the night. They both didn't sleep at all. They held each other and made each other feel safe for as long as they could, knowing it could all come to an end soon. At what would have been the break of dawn - if it wasn't for the blackened sky - Greene got up and made herself a cup of coffee. She stood in the kitchen, naked as the day she was born, leaning over the counter. She sipped at her coffee. Len came in and held her from behind. He wrapped his arms around her waist and rested his chin on her collar. She held the warm cup against her breast and basked in the tender moment.

"Shall I make us breakfast?" he asked.

"Sure… if you want to?"

He spryly jumped to it, grabbing a frying pan out of the cabinet and picking four eggs from the fridge. Greene just stood at the side and watched him. She looked at his body glimmer in the lights as he moved. He wasn't in particularly good shape as he didn't feel he had much need to workout. But he was tall, lean, and confident in himself, and Greene found herself getting increasingly more and more attracted to him each second she looked at him. He glided around the kitchen, strutting as he scrambled the eggs. He didn't bother to put on any clothes. He liked that she was watching him.

Greene sat on a barstool and rested her elbows on the counter and felt the warmth of the cup between her palm. She closed her eyes and she felt happy. She just listened to Len in the kitchen, there were sounds of sizzling coming from a pan. A moment later, he placed two plates of scrambled eggs on toast in front of her on the counter. He pushed one over to her and he sat down next to her and they ate together.

"I had a great time last night, I'm glad we did that," she said.

"Me too," he said.

"Good. Do you think we'll do this again after tonight?"

"What, the sex?" he asked jokingly.

"I don't know what I'm asking. I just don't want you to hate me for going through with this."

"Why would I hate you?"

"You seemed upset last night when I told you about the plan."

"And I was. But now I'm not. Yes, I think it's dangerous and reckless and it's probably going to end in someone getting hurt. But, I'll support you in any way you need. I'm going to be there for you regardless of how I feel about it."

"Thanks."

"So to answer your question, yes! I think we'll do this again after it's all done."

"Good, I'd like that."

They finished eating breakfast together and they talked about nothing in particular. Greene's phone rang on the counter then so did Len's from the coffee table. She quickly answered hers and he went over to the table to answer his.

"Yeah," she said. "Alright, I'm on my way."

She hung up then Len came back over.

"Shall we carpool?" he asked.

"Ah… best not. I've got to pick up Alex after school later anyway. It's the last day of the term."

"Good for her… so I'll meet you there?"

"Yeah, sounds good. I won't be long."

He dressed quickly, gave her a tender kiss on the cheek, and left. She went over to the sofa and sat motionless for a while before getting up and getting herself ready for the day to come. It was just like any other workday - She had a shower, got dressed in her grey suit, put her hair in a ponytail, attached her holster and badge to her belt, and left her apartment.

She drove to the town centre. It was quiet, as the town usually was at this time. She passed the Colossal Squid and briefly saw Roland outside in the alley unloading crates of bottles from his van. She parked just out front of King's Bookstore and Emporium. Len was already inside with Officer Garland, a very short and stocky man in his fifties who never bothered to surpass his rank. They were talking to Gareth O'Brien, the proprietor, who was standing behind the counter.

Greene stopped by the front door and noticed the shattered windows. Broken glass was littered over the sidewalk and even more filled the entrance to the store. She looked in and saw the destruction that had been caused. Books were scattered over the floor. Bent and torn. Ornaments and figurines hailing from every fictitious realm lay cracked and splintered. She stepped inside and Len turned and looked at her.

"Thank god you're here," he said, turning to her.

"Um, excuse me? Are ye listening to me, sonny?" O'Brien said.

Len turned back to the frazzled shopkeeper. "Yes, sorry. Detective Greene is here now so you should speak with her. I'm just the tech."

Greene walked up to the counter, taking care not to step on anything. "Mr. O'Brien, is that right?" she said.

"That's right, miss. I remember you from the beach on that awful day."

"Of course." She looked around the ransacked shop. "What happened here?"

"Damned hooligans broke in last night and stole all the money from the register. They also took the model ship I kept in the case behind me, see?" He turned around and pointed at the broken and empty display case sitting on the cabinet behind him.

"I see," she said, taking out her notebook to write it all down. "Was the ship valuable?"

"Was it valuable?" he scoffed. "It was an heirloom. My father gave it to me and his father gave it to him. It was a model of the USS Constitution."

Greene nodded then looked up and saw the security camera sitting in the ceiling corner. "Does that work?" she asked, pointing at it.

He turned around to see what she meant. "Oh that… it sure does!"

"That's good! Can I take a look at last night's footage?"

"Oh, yes. I don't have no television. But I can get you the tape?"

"Yes, please."

"Course, I'll get ye that right now."

"Thank you. That'll be a big help."

There was a narrow door behind the counter that led to the office. O'Brien went into the back of the store for a moment then came back out holding a video cassette. He handed it to her.

"Thanks again, Mr. O'Brien. If you'd like to give Officer Garland here a complete list of what was stolen, we'll work on getting it all back to you."

"Alrighty," he said.

Greene walked over to Len who was perusing the bookshelves at the back of the store.

"Found anything interesting?" she asked.

120

"This place has everything! I just found a first edition of Dune. I have got to come here more often."

"I meant fingerprints, evidence, that sort of thing?"

"Oh," he laughed. "No, nothing yet. I'll get on it."

"I've got the security footage so I'll head to the station and check it out."

"Okay, I'll catch up later."

She gave him a thumbs up and left him to his work. Officer Garland and O'Brien were busy discussing the ins and outs of model ship building. She left and drove to the station. When she got there, she popped her head into the Captain's office.

"Captain, I've got a security tape to examine, is the viewing room free?"

He raised his head from his paperwork, "Just go and check," he said before bowing his head and returning to his papers.

She nodded and walked down to the viewing room. It was a small, cramped room with an old TV cabinet in the centre. She turned on the lights and then turned on the TV. She put the video tape into the built-in player, rewound it, and then pressed play. She grabbed a chair that was nearby and sat in front of the TV. The tape began at 6pm yesterday when the shop closed. She fast-forwarded the tape and waited for something - or anything - to happen. It wasn't until 4:30am that the burglary occurred. The window shattered and a brick flew through the store and hit the shelf at the back, knocking a whole shelf of books onto the floor. There was no alarm and the streets were empty so nobody heard it. Two men dressed in nothing that anybody would think suitable for a robbery entered through the broken window. One of them jumped the counter and went straight for the cash register, prying it open with a pocket knife and pulling out handfuls of cash. The other searched the cabinets and display cases for anything of value. He broke open several, taking the rare comic books and models that sat inside. At one point the man behind the counter looked up at the camera, his face clearly visible. He was young, could've been as young as sixteen. He could be seen shouting something to his accomplice before jumping back over the counter and leaving the store. The other man didn't leave straight away, he spotted the model ship behind the counter and quickly shattered the glass case with a hammer that he had tucked under his jacket. He took the small, but valuable heirloom. His face could also be seen. He then left after his friend.

"I swear criminals are getting dumber," Greene said to herself.

She rewound the tape to when their faces were clear and she took out her cell phone and took photos of each of them. She left the room with the tape and went to her office and sat at her desk. She plugged her phone into her computer and uploaded the photos she took. She then ran their faces through the local databases. There were instant matches for both. Both of the burglars had driver's licenses.

"Matthew Sanderson, aged sixteen years. And Patrick Limehouse, aged seventeen years. Both high school seniors…" She chuckled. "This was way too easy."

She leaned back in her chair and put her hands behind her head. She relaxed and wished every case were as simple as this. She unplugged her phone and rang the local high school.

"Hi, this is Detective Greene with the Piscator Bay Police Department. Do you have a Matthew Sanderson and a Patrick Limehouse in today?"

"I can check," the school receptionist said. *"No, they both called in sick today. I can give you their contact information if that'll help?"*

"Yes, it would, thank you very much."

The receptionist gave Greene the numbers and addresses of both students. Greene hung up and then contacted Officer Garland over the radio and gave him the younger boy's address. He told her that he and his partner would head over there straight away.

She left the station and made her way to the Limehouse residence. They were a prominent family that lived in a large beachfront home on the north side of town. She parked up the drive and walked down the paved brick path to the front door. She knocked on the door.

A woman opened the door. "Hello, can I help you?" she said.

Greene lifted her badge up. "I'm Detective Greene, are you Mrs. Limehouse?"

"Yes… I am. What's this about?" she said nervously.

"Is your son, Patrick, home today?"

"He's upstairs, in his room. Can you tell me what this is about?"

"There was a break-in at King's Bookstore in the early hours of this morning. The security footage clearly showed that Patrick was one of the two involved."

"Oh god," she said. Her expression changed from concern to disappointment. "Do you want me to bring him down?"

"Yes, I think that would be best."

The mother charged upstairs. Red with anger. Greene remained in the doorway and listened to the sounds emanating from the floor above her. She heard stamping and muffled yelling. The stamping moved further away then back again. The mother came back downstairs with her son in tow. He looked awful and was barely able to stand on his own. She dragged him by his wrist and placed him in front of Greene.

"What did I do?" he bleated incoherently.

His mother slapped him on the back of the head. "Show some respect!" she ordered.

"Patrick, we have video evidence of you and Matt Sanderson breaking into the bookstore last night, I'm going to need you to come down to the station with me to answer some questions," Greene said.

He didn't say anything.

"Will that be necessary? Do you have to take him to the station?" Mrs. Limehouse asked.

Greene looked at her then back at him, "I'm afraid so. Look, this is your first offense so you'll likely get off with doing some community service, maybe a fine. It won't be too bad, as long as you cooperate. Alright?"

It wasn't clear if he heard or even understood anything she just said but he nodded anyway.

"Alright then," Greene said, "Let's go. Since you're a minor, you'll need a parent or guardian to accompany you. Will that be a problem?"

"I'll come, let me just grab my coat," Mrs. Limehouse said.

The three of them went back to the station. Patrick looked pale - like he was going to be sick - for the whole drive. He and his mother were taken to one of the two interrogation rooms. Not long later Officer Garland came in with Matt Sanderson - who looked even worse off than Patrick - and his father and put them in the room opposite.

Greene went back to the Captain's office and informed him that the two had been brought in. He left his office with her and they stood in the hall.

"Nice work, Greene," he said. "Have you been able to retrieve the stolen goods?"

"Not yet, I'm sure they're just lying around in their rooms. I can go do that now."

"Don't worry about it, I'll put Garland and Park on it."

"You sure? I really don't mind, there isn't much else going on."

"I'm sure. If you want something to do, you can go back and inform Mr. O'Brien that we've caught the two responsible and we'll have his items returned to him soon."

"Okay, I'll do that. What about the interrogations?"

"I think I'll handle that myself. I'll put the fear of God into them. I do enjoy doing that."

Greene smiled then chuckled. "Those poor boys."

She left him and went back to her car. The sky had cleared just enough for the sun to shine through. She looked up at the sky and saw a gull flying over the town, the sun shining between the feathers on its wings. She squinted at the rays of warm sun that reached out to her. The clouds returned as quick as they left. Returning the town to the monotone shadow of itself.

The bookstore was still in shambles when she arrived. Gareth O'Brien was busy sweeping the shards of broken glass off the floor into a pan. Greene stepped carefully over the remaining shards into the store. O'Brien stopped what he was doing and greeted her kindly.

"Detective, have ye caught the bastards?" he said.

"We've brought two boys in for questioning. We're confident that they're the ones responsible."

"Good news! Boys you say, young fellas are they?"

"Yeah, sixteen and seventeen years old."

"Such a shame."

"I just came to tell you that we should have your belongings returned to you soon."

"That's a relief. Look, I remember when I was a youth, I certainly did some stupid shit—"

"Didn't we all," Greene said.

"As long as I get my stuff back and my shop gets fixed up, I don't think the boys should be punished too harshly. Is that possible?"

"I don't think that'll be a problem, you can also refuse to press charges, although that doesn't mean the state won't. Eh, I doubt it'll be an issue."

"That's good. Thanks for coming back to tell me. I'll just get back to my cleaning now."

"Alright, you have a good day."

"You too."

They waved goodbye to each other and she went on her way.

❖ ❖ ❖

The rest of the day was uneventful. Greene returned to the station and spoke to the Chief once more. He told her the interrogations of the two boys were a success and they were able to retrieve all of the stolen goods. He also told her that the boys were going to be let off with community service, which included helping Mr. O'Brien fix up his shop. Greene was pleased it was resolved so easily and without fuss.

She sat at her desk and completed paperwork on the burglary until 2:45pm when she left to pick Alex up from school. The weather remained miserable. The constant barrage of rain continued to come down on the small town. She waited outside the school in her parked car. She could see other parents, also in their cars, waiting until the very last moment to leave. The bell rang, and the children ran out as if their lives depended on them getting out of there. All were excited for the Summer break.

Greene left her car and entered the school grounds. She passed the short open iron gate and a stampede of excited children ran past her. Alex stood at the top of the steps to the school, she saw her mother below and waved at her. She was wearing a pink puffer jacket and she had the hood pulled over her head. Paul stood behind her, making sure he remained under the shelter of the eaves. Alex ran down the steps to her mom and hugged her, they both waved goodbye to Paul, and he waved back then went inside.

"What would you like to do? Last day of school, we should do something special to celebrate," Greene said while buckling her daughter into her car seat.

"I want a hot chocolate!"

"Oh, do you now?"

"Yeah!" she said, with a huge smile.

"Alright then, let's get you a hot chocolate."

They didn't have to drive far to get to the café. It was a small boutique place near the town square, filled with tables topped with floral tablecloths and vases of Spring flowers. It was a charming little place and not very busy. They entered and sat down at a table by the window. The young and perky server came over with her notepad.

"Hiya, what can I get you both?" she said.

"Two hot chocolates, please," Greene said.

Alex smiled and laughed.

"Will that be all?" the waitress asked. She smiled at Alex.

"Yes, thanks!" Greene said.

The waitress left and came back a couple of minutes later with two hot chocolates in fancy cups with two marshmallows each on the side of the saucer. "Enjoy!" she said.

They sat and sipped at their hot chocolates. Greene had to remind Alex to blow on it before taking a sip. The strong winds outside pushed the rain on an angle and it hit the windows with force. Alex wasn't afraid, in fact, she quite liked the stormy weather. Greene on the other hand found it unsettling, as if it were a bad omen sending her a warning not to go through with tonight's plan.

She took Alex straight home afterwards. Alex rang the doorbell - as she liked to do - and Paul came to the door and welcomed them both inside. Alex ran straight up to her room with her backpack in tow.

"Would you like something to drink?" Paul asked.

"We just had hot chocolates."

"Sounds nice."

"It was." She checked her watch, it was almost 5pm already. The time had passed quick. "I'm sorry, I can't stay."

"Oh, that's alright. Do you have work?"

"Yeah, it's been a very busy week. Um, say goodbye to Alex for me, will you? And tell her I love her?"

"Of course… Meredith, is everything alright?"

"Yeah, everything's fine. Nothing to worry about."

She went back outside and stepped onto the porch. Paul followed her out.

"Same time again on Monday?" she asked.

"Sure, but there's no school so feel free to come around any time, okay?"

"Alright then, I'll let you know."

She went back to her car and watched Paul go back inside. She hoped she'd see them again. It was almost time. She took out her phone and called Lipton who was at home preparing for the night ahead.

Lipton sat on a simple wooden chair in his basement and stared at the walls. He studied the photos of the Pentaghasts, the courtroom transcripts, and the pictures of the dead girls. This was the night, he thought, that it was all going to end. He was anxious and excited, hopeful and worried all at once. He stood up and walked over to the cabinet hidden underneath the staircase. He opened it up, pulled both doors wide open, and took a step back. Inside the cabinet was an arsenal. Rifles of every calibre lined up in unison. Handguns and knives hung on the inside of the doors. Boxes of ammunition filled up the space between. He picked up the duffle bag that lay on the floor beside his chair and began to fill it with anything and everything he thought he may need. He loaded into the bag a pump action shotgun, an assault rifle, two handguns, enough ammunition to last, and a serrated combat knife. Finally, he threw in two Kevlar vests. He closed the cabinet doors and opened the drawer underneath. Inside were several piles of cash, all neatly stacked. He took all of it and threw it in the zipped side-pocket of the bag. The bag was unbelievably heavy that even he struggled to lift it. He dragged it upstairs to the living room and left it on the floor by the front door. He went to his fridge and grabbed himself a can of beer and sat himself down on the couch and drank it slowly as he watched the clock tick above his fireplace.

His phone rang. He looked at it and saw that it was Greene calling. He answered.

"Yeah," he said.

"Hi, are you ready?" she said.

"Yeah, are you?"

"I hope so. I'm going to head to the club now."

"Okay, I'll be there shortly. I'll bring some equipment. Just a few essentials."

"Okay, I'll see you soon," she said. She hung up.

He put his phone away, closed his eyes, and breathed out slowly then breathed in again. He repeated this over and over again several times then he finished his beer and placed the empty can on his coffee table.

He left his house on the hill and put the duffle bag in the trunk of his car. He got in and drove down into town before making a turn-off towards the port. When he arrived at the club, he pulled around into the back alley, near the backdoor. Greene was already there, waiting beside her car. He parked next to her.

"Are you sure you're ready for this?" he asked her as he got out of his car.

"Yes," she said confidently. "Are you?"

He went round to the trunk and opened it up and pulled out the duffle bag. He held the heavy bag up with both hands. "I'm ready!" he said.

The backdoor opened and a man came out. It was dark and they both looked at him but couldn't recognize him.

"Mr. Cartwright told me to come get you," he said.

"And who are you?" Lipton asked. He squinted but couldn't make out his face.

The man stepped into the light. "I'm Freddie, Mr. Cartwright's head of security," he said.

Lipton turned to Greene. "The hell does he need a head of security for?" he asked.

Greene shrugged then walked up to Freddie. Lipton followed after her and the three of them entered the club. They were led through the empty back corridors down to a secluded room. A woman was in the room waiting for them. She was tall and wore a bright red ballgown that showed off her figure.

"Hi," the woman said, giving them a little uncertain wave.

"Hello," Greene said. "I take it you're the one who's supposed to help me get ready?"

"That's right!" she said. She looked at Lipton. "Is he going to stay?"

Greene looked back at Lipton and Freddie. "You two can wait outside," she said.

"Oh, yeah, sure thing," Lipton said. He and Freddie both left the room and stood in the dark corridor.

Greene locked the door behind them. "So, how do we do this?" she asked the woman.

The woman turned around and went over to a rack of clothes. She looked through them until she came to the blue dress. "Aha," she said, "this is it!" She took the dress off the rack and went back over to Greene. "Well, come on then. Get undressed."

"Oh... of course. Do you mind turning around?"

"Darlin', I'm here to help you dress. I'm going to see everything."

"Right…"

"Do you need help?"

"No, that's okay." Greene started undressing, first taking off her jacket and shirt then her boots, socks, and pants. She stood in her underwear, trying to cover herself with her hands.

"And the bra?" the woman said.

"Sorry," Greene said. She removed her bra, and then she used her right arm to cover herself.

"No need to be shy, I've got them too. Now hop in." She knelt down with the dress ready for Greene to step into it.

Greene stepped into the dress and the woman lifted it up to her breasts. She gave it a shimmy to make sure everything was fitted properly. The woman stepped around her and zipped it up at the back then she took a step back and eyed her from head to toe.

"It fits you just right," she said.

Greene saw the bandaged wound on her arm, fully visible. "I'll need to cover that," she said, pointing it out to the woman.

"Oh, I see. We have some evening gloves that should cover it. I'll go get them."

The woman returned with a pair of long, black gloves and handed them to Greene.

Greene slid on the gloves and walked over to the nearby full-body mirror and looked at herself. The gloves stretched up close to her shoulders and completely covered the bandages. It was as if it never happened. She smiled looking at herself. She looked more beautiful than she had ever thought possible. The dress flowed perfectly down to her calves and it sat comfortably around her curves, accentuating her breasts and her hips. She felt ready for anything.

The woman stood behind her, she nodded approvingly and put her hands on the sides of Greene's shoulders. "It's perfect!" she said. "I'll go and let your friend in." She went and opened the door and asked them to enter.

Lipton wasn't standing alone with Freddie anymore. Freddie had left, and Len had arrived and was waiting in the hall next to him. They both came in and saw Greene standing there in all her beauty.

"Not bad," Lipton said. He placed the duffle bag on the couch on the other side of the room.

Len walked up to her, "You look incredible," he said.

"I just have to do her hair and makeup and we'll be all good to go," the woman said. She walked over to the vanity in the corner and pulled out the chair. Greene sat down and the woman began. She let down Greene's ponytail and combed it. She fluffed her hair a little to give it some body. "That'll do, I guess. What do you think?" she asked.

"It looks good," Greene said.

The woman then gave her face a makeover. Nothing extravagant, just some foundation and a little blush. "There... done," she said.

Greene turned around in her chair, "What do you think?" she said.

Len's mouth was agape. He didn't say anything, he only nodded.

Lipton didn't seem to care. "You look fine," he said, "should work." He picked up the dufflebag from the couch and brought it over to her. He opened it up and rummaged around until he found it. He pulled out a small handgun, just a modest .22 pistol and its holster. He took a strap from the side compartment and attached it to the holster. He looked up at Greene. "We'll put this around your thigh, just in case," he said.

Greene nodded.

Lipton looked up at Len, "You want to do the honors?" he said.

Len came over and grabbed the holster from him and knelt in front of her and lifted her dress over her knees. He then wrapped the holster around her right thigh, making sure it was positioned in such a way that it was easily accessible, but not noticeable. He looked up at her. She was looking down at him with a half smile that seemed almost sad.

"Let me just go and get your shoes," the woman said.

"Okay, all done," Len said, pulling her dress back down.

"Len and I will be right behind you, don't you worry," Lipton said. "We'll be with you every step. We're ending this tonight."

The woman came back over with the shoes and put them on Greene's feet. They were jet black and high-heeled. Elegant. Once they were fitted Greene wiggled her feet back and forth to make sure they wouldn't tear at her heels. She was startled when the door opened once again and Errol Cartwright came waltzing in.

"We're preparing to leave. You 'ave five minutes," he said.

"Oh, Christ," Greene muttered anxiously under her breath.

"It's okay if you can't go through with this," Len said, holding her hand. "We can call the Captain—"

"No, we can't," Lipton said. "This is it. This is our only chance to end this once and for all. There's no going back now… and you don't have to worry, we'll be with you the whole time, you'll be fine."

"Okay," she said.

"Here," Lipton said. He walked over to her and put an earpiece in her right ear. "Now you can hear us and we'll be able to hear you. Just flip that switch on its side to turn it on when you need to use it, okay? We'll be with you."

"Thanks! Okay…" She took a deep breath. "I'm ready."

He nodded.

Cartwright stood in the doorway and made a flailing gesture with his arms. "Come on, we've got to go," he said with urgency.

◆ ◆ ◆

They watched the girls who were queued outside the club get into the black work van one by one. Greene was third from the back and she didn't look out of place. Half of the girls looked barely old enough to drink - they smiled at Freddie as he gave them a hand and loaded them on board - and the other half looked like their lives were ones filled without hope. Greene disappeared into the van.

"I'm worried. Are you sure she'll be able to handle this?" Len asked.

"She's tough and she knows what to do, don't worry, she can handle herself just fine," Lipton said. He turned on the engine and put the car into gear, preparing to follow the van to wherever it may go.

Greene sat in the dark and cramped van. There were a dozen girls in total, six on each side of the van. They were all dressed extravagantly as if they were about to be presented to royalty. The woman who helped Greene get dressed sat beside her. She was applying a deep red lipstick that matched her gown. Greene leaned over to her. "What's your name?" she whispered.

"They call me Pearl," the woman whispered back.

"And your real name?"

"Jen."

"I'm Meredith. Have you done this before?"

"A couple of times. It's not too bad."

The van began to move, and the drive to the lodge was long. After a while, no other traffic could be heard. Over an hour had passed and Greene was beginning to feel anxious, and she could feel the sweat forming on her. The road suddenly became bumpy and uneven and soon after the van slowed to a crawl.

Lipton kept a modest distance to the van, despite the fact that Errol and Freddie knew they were following them. He knew how he wanted this night to end and didn't want to risk anything complicating it. The van moved through the wooded landscape down a deserted country road. The torrential rain kept coming down as if God had planned a second flood. The van slowed and stopped just short of a large wooden gate. Freddie leaned out of the window and waved at a camera above the fence. The gate opened for them.

Lipton and Len parked the car two hundred feet from the gate and watched the van enter. It disappeared from their sight for a moment before returning to view. It parked in front of the lodge. It was a large wooden building built far away, hidden from the surrounding world. Calling it a lodge was a gross understatement. Lipton held up his binoculars and watched the van be emptied. The women were then led through the front entrance into the lodge.

"Here we go," Lipton said.

The inside of the lodge was lit by candles, resting high above them and housed in grand chandeliers. Greene followed the girls in front of her. They were being led through the main foyer down to the parlour room at the rear. She observed the guards that stood around them, most of whom wore black suits and had handguns visible in holsters under their arms. Once in the parlour, all the women were lined up in a single row. At least thirty men were waiting in the room for them. They sat comfortably and gazed upon them.

"You know the drill, gentlemen. Pick who you like, and enjoy yourselves," said an impish voice coming from above.

Greene looked over to the man who was speaking. It was Lyle, standing proudly away from the crowd at the top of the staircase at the side of the room. The men on the sofas and lounge chairs stood up and began mingling with the women. Some of the men had already chosen who they fancied and they drifted out of the room in pairs. Greene noticed a man looking at her. He was an average-looking older man with greying hair and square glasses. He looked harmless. She remained composed as he walked over to her.

"Hi, would you like to come with me?" he asked in a kind but unsettling manner.

"Sure," Greene said with a fake smile.

He put his arm around her waist and they walked out of the parlour. She looked back up at Lyle - standing above everyone else as if he were a king, grinning smugly - as they left. He led her down the main hall and they turned to the right. Greene looked around the large building, taking note of the layout, and potential exits. They went down a long corridor lined with rooms. The majority of the doors remained open for all who wished to see. She peeked into one as they passed. An old man was sitting on the bed naked, caressing himself. The young woman with him was in the middle of undressing in front of him. The man escorting Greene stopped in front of the doorway and looked in.

"We can stay and watch if you'd like?" he said.

Greene looked away from them. "No, thanks," she said politely.

They continued down the corridor. Greene peered into each room they passed. Most weren't shocking to her - women on their knees giving blowjobs, or the men using their hands on them - she expected worse. They stopped outside an empty room.

"This is our room," the man said.

He showed her inside. It was a small room, with a bed and not much else. There was an ensuite bathroom at the side. He shut the door behind them. The door shutting made a bang that frightened Greene that she jumped slightly and put her hand over her heart.

"Don't be scared," the man said.

"I'm not," she said.

All the windows were bolted shut. There was no other way out.

"Sit on the bed," he said.

She hesitated. She knew that she had to make an excuse to get out of the room. The longer she was there, the more danger she was in. The man sat on the edge of the bed and patted the mattress beside him.

"Come here," he said.

"I really should go freshen up," she said.

"That's not necessary, I'm sure you're fine. Now, come sit down."

Greene walked over to him slowly and sat beside him. There was no way she was going to let him touch her, but she couldn't make a scene or alert the security or this all would have been for nothing. The man shuffled closer to her. He leaned in close and sniffed her neck. She shivered with discomfort.

"You smell good," he said, "do you want to touch me?"

He put his hand on his crotch and squeezed.

"No, thank you!" Greene said bluntly.

"No? Why not? Oh, I see. You want me to do the work, is that it?"

He slid off the bed and knelt next to her. He put his hand on her right knee and slowly moved it up her leg.

"No!" Greene shouted.

She grabbed his hand and pushed it away from her. His face turned red. She reached up her thigh and pulled the gun from its holster and stood up and aimed it down at him. He fell backwards onto the floor with his hand raised.

"What the hell are you doing?" he said.

Greene looked around and saw a rack of various apparatuses on the wall. There were whips and chains. Gags and cages. There was a long coil of rope.

"Grab that rope!" she ordered.

He quickly raised himself off the floor and skipped over to the rack and grabbed the rope.

"Now lie down on your front!"

He did what he was told. He lay down and she took the rope from his hand and tied the rope around his arms, then around his feet. He laid hogtied on the floor. She grabbed the gag from the rack and placed it in his mouth. He struggled but couldn't do anything to get free. She stood and looked down at him wriggling around like a worm, trying to shout through the gag. His eyes watering. She knelt down next to him and looked him in the eye. He looked pathetic in his immobility. She gripped her gun firmly and smacked him in the side of the head with the butt of the handle. His head split open and a narrow river of blood came pouring out, soaking his left eye, and dripping onto the wooden floor.

"That's the least you deserve, you piece of shit!" she said.

His eyelids flickered then he fell into unconsciousness.

She put her gun back into the holster under her dress, and then she moved over to the door. She put her ear up to the door and listened. The corridor sounded empty but she could hear moaning and screaming coming from the other rooms. She slowly opened the door just enough to get a peek outside. The corridor was deserted. She looked back at the man lying tied up on the floor. She knew it wouldn't be long until he was found so she'd have to be quick. She stepped into the hall, turned left, and made her way down. Each room she passed had a cornucopia of human sexuality on display. She never looked. At the end of the hall was a junction, she looked down to the left and saw a door at the end that looked like it led outside. She went up to the door and looked out the window. The window was stained so she couldn't make out anything that was outside. The door was unlocked. She opened it but before she could step into the cold, rainy night, she heard footsteps behind her. She lowered her hand down and reached under her dress for the holster. She swiftly pulled out the pistol and turned around and aimed it at the encroaching man.

"Fuckin' hell!" Cartwright said, raising his hands up. "It's me. Would you kindly lower the gun?"

Greene let out a relieved sigh at the sight of the little man and lowered her gun.

"Why would you sneak up on me like that, are you trying to get yourself shot?" she said.

"I called your name several times, don't call me stupid just because you're half deaf. I see you've found a way out, that's good. Come on, I'll show you how to get to the gate from 'ere."

They stepped outside into the rain and he gave her explicit instructions on how to reach the gate. It wasn't too far away and he said it would be easy to find. He told her to 'just follow the fence'.

"What are you going to do?" she asked him.

Cartwright scoffed. "I'm getting Freddie and getting the fuck outta 'ere before you and your friend bring the wrath of god down upon that prick," he said. "Always wanted to go down to Florida and see an alligator. Might as well do that while I still can. I'd say it's been a pleasure, but I'd be lyin'."

He went back inside and that was the last she saw of him.

Lipton was already waiting at the side gate that Cartwright told them about. There was an easy-to-follow path that led through the woods from the road. He had his duffle bag on the ground and he was preparing the weapons, making sure they were all loaded. He threw on one of the Kevlar vests and tightened the straps around his chest and waist. He picked up the assault rifle, it was an HK416 with an attached night vision scope and laser sight. Excessive in every respect. He was determined to end this for good, by whatever means necessary.

Greene ran across the grounds from the lodge, westerly towards the gate. It didn't take long for her dress to become crumpled and wet, and for her hair to be drenched. She ran past an old decrepit barn, and a solar power generator - its incessant hum deafening. She kept running until she could no longer see the lodge behind her. She was soon surrounded by woods, large pine trees stretched up as high as she could see, disappearing into the darkness. She made it to the fence. It was a tall steel chainlink fence with three rows of barbed wire layering the top. She looked to her left and then to her right. She was unsure of which way to go. She switched on her earpiece and tapped it three times.

"Lipton, can you hear me?" she said.

"I hear you," he said.

"I'm at the fence, but I don't see the gate."

Lipton pulled out his knife from his belt and tapped the fence.

"Do you hear that?" he said.

"What?"

He hit the fence harder.

"Yes, I hear it!" she said.

The clanking of steel was faint, but the sound vibrated down the fence. She followed it to her right. She walked along the fence line until she saw him standing on the other side, clad in black. She reached the gate. It was a solid steel door surrounded by the chain link. It had a simple bolt lock, unreachable from the other side. She grabbed and pulled it to the side, unhinging it from its sheathe. She pulled the door by the handle, and it swung open with ease. She stepped through.

Lipton looked at Greene. Her dress was muddy and soaked, and her makeup had run down her face. He knelt down and pulled Greene's coat from his duffle bag.

"Thought you'd need this," he said. He handed her the coat and she threw it over her shoulders.

"Thanks," she said. "What do we do now?"

She hadn't yet noticed the rifle strapped to his back.

"Right now, you need to head down this path, it leads back to the road. Len's waiting for you. You'll be safe there. I'm going in."

"What are you talking about? You can't go in alone!"

"I can, and I will. And don't you try to follow me. Just leave and I'll finish this for both of us."

She finally got a good look at him. She saw the armour he wore and the weapons on his person. He looked like he was prepared for war.

"What are you going to do?" she said.

"I'm going to end this."

"You're going to kill him, aren't you?"

"If it comes to that, yes, I will."

"Lipton, no! You can't!"

"Just leave, Greene. Go home."

He pushed past her and stepped through the gate.

"No," she said. "I can't let you do this."

He turned back and looked at her, "I've been waiting for an opportunity like this to come along for a long, long time. I won't let you get in my way. I am sorry," he said. He quickly shut the gate door and locked it. She ran up to it and pushed and tried to force it open.

"Lipton!" she yelled from behind the impenetrable gate. "Open the gate, now! Daniel!"

He turned away from her and walked out into the woods, towards the lodge. He disappeared behind the shimmer of rain and blackness. She called out to him once more, and then she ran back through the woods towards the road.

Len was waiting in the car. He watched the main entrance to the lodge with keen eyes. A guard would occasionally come into view from one side of the large gate, then disappear again past the other. Out of the corner of his eye, he saw movement. It frightened him and he turned sharply and saw Greene running out of the woods. She stopped at the road and looked to her left, at the gate. She then turned back to Len and kept on running towards him. She reached the car and opened the passenger door and got in and closed it gently.

"What happened, are you okay?" he asked.

She sat shivering. "Y-yeah I-I'm fine," she said, pulling her coat tight.

"Where's Lipton?"

137

"H-he went in."

"What? Alone?"

"He didn't give me much choice."

"I'm calling this in," he said. "This has gotten out of hand."

"Yeah, you're right, this was a mistake. Do it."

◆ ◆ ◆

Lipton crept up to the lodge. He held his silenced pistol to his chest, ever ready. He made his way across the grounds, past the barn, and went up to a window and peered inside. He saw a man lying on the bed, with a woman straddling atop of him while another man sat in a chair in the corner of the room watching.

He crouched back down below the window and slowly moved down the side of the building and stopped at a door. This was the same side door Greene had used to leave. He looked through the small frosted window and saw nothing stirring beyond. He heard the loud creaking sound of the main gate open. He looked over and saw Cartwright's black van pull out and vanish out of the compound.

He turned back to the door, and slowly and gently turned the brass doorknob and pushed the door quietly open. He removed his muddy boots and placed them by the door as he entered. He unstrapped the rifle on his back and placed it against the wall by his boots. He felt he wouldn't have much use for it in such tight quarters. He held his pistol up to his chin, and then he moved down the hall. Entering the monolithic building gave a distinct feeling of stepping back to a simpler and harsher time. Only the sounds of the patrons' carnality could be heard down the halls of the lodge. Lipton moved through the corridors, briefly peeking into each room he passed and quickly moving on to the next. He saw acts of intimacy and depravity that only the adventurous few would understand.

He heard the sounds of two people conversing ahead of him. Moving closer. He sidestepped into the room closest to him. He quickly closed the door and listened through the door. The radio was playing in the room. Light jazz filled the room with a pleasant ambience.

"Who are you?" said a voice coming from behind him, inside the room. "Get out of here!"

Lipton turned around and saw a skinny, naked man sitting on the bed. The man shielded his crotch with his hands and then noticed the gun that Lipton wielded. The man raised one hand in the air.

"Oh fuck! Please don't hurt me!" he said.

Lipton raised a single finger up to his lips.

The man nodded.

Lipton pressed his ear to the door again and heard footsteps and muffled speech go by and then there was silence. Lipton turned to the man on the bed and aimed his pistol at him.

"No, please…" the man said, "I've got money, lots of money. It's all yours, okay? Just don't kill me."

"What's your name?"

"P-Pat," the man said.

Lipton nodded and smiled. "I recognize your voice… from the radio. Pat Mallory. That's you, am I right?"

"Yes! Yes, that's me!"

"Do you know Lyle Pentaghast?"

"What? Uh, sort of. He owns this place. This is his… event."

"And do you know where he is right now?"

"T-The main suite—"

"Is that a guess?"

"No, I'm sure. He'll be there."

Lipton took a step toward Mallory and made sure he saw the gun again.

"Upstairs," Mallory said, pointing up. "Go right down the hall and there will be a staircase in the main parlor, can't miss it. You won't kill me, will you?"

"You've been very helpful," Lipton said dryly.

Lipton raised his pistol, aiming it at the whimpering Mallory sitting there on the bed, naked and vulnerable. Mallory raised both hands ever so slightly before Lipton pulled the trigger. Everything seemed to move in slow motion. The bullet expelled out the back of Mallory's head and hit the wooden headboard behind him - cracking and splitting through the wood - and a geyser of blood followed and painted the bedding red. The sound of the suppressed gunshot was further muffled by the music playing from the radio. He hoped it was enough. Lipton lowered the gun and turned around and saw the door handle wiggle. He quickly moved behind the door as it opened. A woman walked in carrying a bucket of ice with both hands. The bucket blocked her view so she hadn't yet seen Mallory lying dead on the bedspread.

Lipton closed the door behind her and grabbed her mouth and put his gun up to the back of her head. "Don't move and don't you say a word," he said. He moved her over to the wall. She still held the bucket of ice tight to her chest as if it were a shield. She saw the body of Mallory lying on the blood-soaked bed and her eyes widened with fear then she shut them tight.

"I won't hurt you," he said. "I'm not here for you."

She kept her eyes shut, and he looked around the room. There was an ensuite in the corner by the door. He led the woman to the bathroom and pushed her inside.

"Stay here for an hour. Don't come out until then. Do you understand?"

She nodded, still holding the bucket of ice in front of her.

He closed the bathroom door, leaving the frightened girl there, and then moved back to the bedroom door. He opened it slowly, peering out into the candlelit hall. There was nobody and nothing out there. The sounds coming from other rooms seemed louder that he couldn't hear much else. He left the room and moved down the hall in the direction of the parlour room. At the end of the hall, he looked to the left and saw the main parlour room and the staircase leading up to Pentaghast's suite. Two men were sitting on the long and twisting, bright red sofa that coiled around the edge of the great room. They were wearing nothing but robes and they were smoking cigars. Lipton waited at the corner and listened to them talk for a moment. They talked about nothing pertinent, just basic small talk. One asked the other if he thought the weather would clear soon and the other replied that he had no idea.

The men finished their cigars and moved on.

Lipton moved deftly into the parlour like a hunter and saw the staircase to his left. He looked up at the top of the stairs and then briskly ascended them. At the top of the stairs, there was a long balcony that wrapped around the foyer. To the right was a hall that led to the main suite. Lipton moved down the corridor, keeping his pistol aimed in front of him. A man stood at the end of the hall, leaning against the wall and looking at the floor. His gun was visible in its holster under his arm. Lipton slowly moved closer to him, never lowering his aim from him. The guard raised his head and turned and saw

Lipton down the hall, and before he could react Lipton fired two shots at the man's chest that threw him back against the wall, then his body slowly seeped down onto the floor.

Lipton didn't stop, he stood at the door and listened. He heard gasping and moaning on the other side. A voice could be heard but he couldn't make out what was said. He tried to open the door but it was locked. He stepped back and kicked the door from its hinges and stepped into the expansive bedroom. A naked woman was tied up on the bed, she was lying on her stomach with her arms and legs tied to each corner of the bed frame. Her back was bleeding and her mouth was gagged and she was crying. She was trying to say something. He recognised her as the woman from the club.

Lipton took a step up to the bed when he felt a sharp jolt in his back. An arm reached around and grabbed his neck then he felt another force of pressure in his back, this one less painful. Lipton twisted and grabbed the arm and pulled it down across his chest and threw the assailant over his shoulder onto the floor. It was Lyle, with a thin blade in his hand. Blood dripping down from it.

Lipton ran his hand over his back and felt the blood seep from the first stab wound. It was deep. The second one landed on the Kevlar. He aimed his pistol at Lyle, who was lying on the floor looking up at him.

"Is that you?" Lyle said to Lipton who was unrecognisable in his black garb.

Lipton kept his aim at him and pulled his balaclava up to his forehead. "So you remember me?" he said.

"I knew you would come. What now? Are you going to kill me? All because of that cop?"

"No, not just because of him. You can add him to the list of reasons why you deserve to die. I'm here because of Jessica Perdeaux, Caitlyn Sommers, Kelly Royce, Liana Jackson, Shauna Ewens, and all the nameless women that you and your father have killed."

The girl on the bed started to twist and pull at her binds.

"You have no proof," Lyle said, still gripping the blade.

"I know… that's why I'm here. That's why I'm doing this."

"You're fucking insane! You won't get away with this!"

"Doesn't matter, my mind is clear."

Lyle used all his strength to push himself off the floor and lunge at Lipton. Lipton fired one shot then another two in quick succession. Each one hit Lyle in the abdomen. The first two in the stomach and the third in the chest. He dropped his knife on the floor and fell backwards onto the bed then bounced off and collapsed onto the floor. He writhed around and wheezed and began to crawl away. His blood created a trail behind him. Lipton walked up to him, still aiming his pistol at the wretched and suffering man. Lyle rolled over and looked up at him. He tried to speak but no words came out, only a gasp and a sputtering of blood that fell over his face. He raised his hand up, begging for a mercy that would never come.

Lipton stared into his eyes and shot the already dying man in the head, expelling skull and brain matter over the bearskin rug and the wooden floor beneath it. The girl on the bed stopped trying to get free of her binds and lay there motionless, crying into the bed sheets. Lipton breathed deeply out as if he'd been holding his breath for a lifetime. He then reholstered his weapon. He looked at the girl on the bed and picked up Lyle's knife off the floor and cut the ropes tying her down. She quickly sat up and shuffled to the other end of the bed and covered her naked self with a pillow.

"It's okay," he said, dropping the knife. "You remember me? I won't hurt you. And he's not going to hurt you anymore." He looked back down at Lyle. "It's over."

Lipton pulled his balaclava back over his face and exited the room. He moved back down the hall to the inner balcony that overlooked the parlour. When he reached the end he looked out past the foyer and out of the large windows that decorated the front wall of the lodge. He saw lights flicker in the distance. The dim shades of red and blue moved across the horizon like shooting stars, edging ever closer.

"Goddamn it," he said.

He ran down the stairs and followed his way back through the winding corridors. He made it to the side door he'd used to enter. He put on his boots and grabbed the rifle. He looked out and to his left, he saw the state police cruisers arrive at the front gate. The security guards at the gate spoke to the troopers through the bars and then opened the gates for them to enter. Lipton headed to the right, back towards the side gate. He ran as fast as he could past the barn and the generator, the cropping of old sheds and disused outhouses, and finally made it back to the woods. He followed the fence down to the gate and unbolted it and went through, picking up his duffle bag which remained where he left it, and then storing the rifle back inside it. He continued on through the woods, descending deeper into the unknown, away from the road and his former colleagues. He knew what he had done was unforgivable, and despite him not regretting any of it, he knew he had only one further course of action to take. One that will finally put an end to all of this. One that will finally grant him peace.

VII

The state police raided the lodge in force, searching through every room and bringing out all the men and women that remained inside. They lined them up on the motor court. The men kneeling on one side and the women on the other. Most unclothed to some degree. Two ambulances showed up soon after and the paramedics treated the injured woman and the man who Greene had subdued. When they brought out the three dead everybody went silent, even those afraid and crying pushed their emotion aside to reflect for a moment.

Greene and Len stood outside the main gates, out of the way of the frantic police presence. A trooper walked up to them.

"You called this in?" she asked.

Greene pulled the coat tighter around her cold shoulders.

"I did," Len said, raising his hand slightly.

"I was told that you're both police?"

"Yes, down in Piscator Bay. I just work forensics and she's a detective."

The trooper looked at Greene, dressed not unlike the myriad of working girls sitting on the pavement mere feet away.

Greene noticed the trooper's confusion. "I was working undercover," she said.

"Uh huh," the trooper mumbled, writing it all down on a notepad.

"We were investigating the murder of a local girl, and we had evidence linking these… parties to the people responsible. I went in to find out what I could."

"And did you find anything?"

"Just that these men deserve to be in prison, that's all."

"Three men are dead—"

"I had already left by then. I can't tell you anything about that."

The trooper put away her notepad. "Alrighty then, my Chief will want to speak to yours."

"I've already called Captain McGovern, and he's on his way here as we speak," Len said.

"Good… that'll be all for now then. Just wait here."

The trooper left them and returned to her colleagues who were busy questioning all the others.

"Three people… fucking hell," Len said quietly. He rubbed his eyes in disbelief.

"I didn't know, I swear I didn't," Greene said. She grabbed his forearm.

He looked at her. "I know you didn't, but still… it wasn't supposed to go this way, how did it all come to this?"

"I know. I'm sorry. What are we going to tell McGovern?"

"The truth. We have to tell him the truth. We can't lie to him about this now. He needs to know."

"I know you're right."

It was nearing dawn and the rain had finally seceded. The stars were bright and clear up in the black sky. Greene looked up in awe at the sky. The moon was faint and hard to see as it was becoming anew. A shooting star flew past it, across the sky.

"Did you see that?" she said, pointing up.

"No, what?" Len said. He was leaning on his car and looked up at where she was pointing.

"A shooting star."

"Better make a wish."

She closed her eyes and thought about what she wanted most. The last week had felt like a deliberate attempt to destroy any hopes for a happy life that she had left. The more she thought about the week's events the more things became clear to her. There was a lot to hate but a lot of good came out of it too. She thought about Len, who before Monday was nothing more than a friendly colleague whom she'd wave hello to while getting her morning coffee. But now he had become much more. She hoped that this night hadn't changed how he felt about her because she knew for certain how she felt about him. She then thought about her relationship with Paul and Alex, and how she felt there was a future there as well, one that gave her much love and joy. Her thoughts about the case were the most confusing to her. She hated everything about the week in regards to the investigation. It brought her nothing but contempt for others and despair for herself. And yet at the same time, she felt proud that they were able to keep fighting in the face of adversity and find out who was responsible and do something to stop them even if it meant doing something unforgivable themselves.

She opened her eyes and looked at Len who was staring at her with his soft, kind eyes. She smiled at him and he smiled back at her and held her hand.

They waited together and not long after, a car pulled up behind theirs and Captain McGovern stepped out and walked over to them. His face frowned and sour.

"What the hell were you two thinking? You should've come to me," he said.

"We know," Greene said. "We're sorry, Captain."

He looked past the gates at the few remaining people still inside. Most of the men and women had either been taken to hospital, into custody, or allowed to leave. The lodge was now quiet.

"Tell me what happened, and don't leave anything out if you wish to keep your jobs?"

"We made an agreement with Errol Cartwright. He organized this party with Lyle Pentaghast…"

McGovern looked furious but didn't interrupt.

"…We knew that Lyle would be here so we arranged for me to go in as one of the girls and when I was in I was to sneak off and unlock the side gate, through the woods there, and let Lipton in—"

"Lipton was here?" McGovern said.

"He was."

"And where is he now?"

"We haven't seen him since he went in."

"And now there are three dead, including Lyle Pentaghast."

"Yes."

"Fuck, Greene."

"I swear to you, sir, we were just supposed to go in and try to bring him in or get a confession or catch him in the act. Something. I didn't know he was going to kill him. I tried to stop him when I discovered his plans but he locked me out and there was nothing more I could do."

"You do realize he'll be done for murder now? Damn it! What could've possessed him?"

Greene shrugged slightly. "I think he was tired of them getting away with it," she said.

"That's no excuse."

"No, I know it's not. But it's an explanation."

"We have DNA samples, all we needed to do was bring him in and compare. Goddamn it!" McGovern rubbed his tired eyes then turned around and looked at the lodge - lit up by the remaining flashing police lights - before turning back to them. "You two should head home. I'll need to coordinate with the state troopers then we can debrief later in the day."

"Yes sir," Greene said. She and Len got into his car and the two of them drove away. Greene watched McGovern head through the gate and speak to the troopers. They drove back through the woodland and over the hills back to town. By the time they arrived, the sun had begun to rise. The cloud had dissipated and the sky was clear and was a bright shade of blue they hadn't seen for a long while.

◆ ◆ ◆

Lipton arrived back at his house just before the crack of dawn. He had no car to get back so he walked for twenty miles to the truckstop that sat in the valley between the hillsides - the same truckstop that he and Greene stopped at three days earlier. It was open all hours and he was able to find a trucker who had stopped for an early morning meal to drive him back to town. The trucker didn't ask him any questions. Lipton just handed the man a small stack of bills from his bag, and the trucker took it gladly. Once he returned to town he entered his home and dropped the duffle bag on the floor by the door and collapsed next to it. He felt the wound in his back. The half-dried blood stuck to his fingers, and the pain was striking. He sat on the floor and rested his tired body.

"I think he's got me," he said. He laughed a little but it hurt too much.

He used his hands to push himself back to his feet then he went into the kitchen. He grabbed a bottle of water from the fridge and drank it all, savouring the last refreshing drop. His body ached and his head throbbed. It took all of his energy to not collapse again from exhaustion. He went and took a pencil and a sheet of paper from the desk in his office by the living room and wrote a letter explaining himself. He put it in an envelope and he wrote 'Greene' on the front of it and went back to the front door.

"I'm sorry," he said as he placed the letter down on the table next to the door.

He picked the duffle bag back up as he left his house for the last time. He sat it down on the back seat of his car then he got in and drove out of town once more. He knew this was it, that this was what he was always meant to do. There was never going to be any justice for those girls. He couldn't rely on the law and the justice system to do what it needed to. These men had been getting away with it for almost forty years and that was never going to change. He had a choice. He could keep banging his head trying to get justice done through the law or go on his own path and deliver justice himself. And with Lyle's death, he had already made his decision.

He drove north, and he kept driving until the town which he had come to love, and call his home, vanished from view. The sun had risen and shone through the window and warmed his cheek. As he passed the hills and entered the wooded valleys, the great pines blocked out the sun and cooled him. He never regretted his actions nor did he doubt what he was about to do. He drove and continued to drive until the sun was clear and full in the bright summer sky. Mount Blue became visible ahead of him like a beacon rising up to guide him. He made it to the country road that led up to the Pentaghast estate. He slowed to the gate, and stopped by the buzzer. He leaned out and pressed the bell.

"What do you want?" asked Adrian the butler through the intercom.

"It's Detective Lipton. I was here a few days ago, I don't know if you remember me. I need to ask Mr. Pentaghast some follow-up questions."

There was a moment of silence then the intercom clicked off and the gates opened. Lipton slowly pulled forward into the great courtyard and parked in front of the manor entrance. The butler came out and waited for him by the doors. Lipton kept a careful watch on him, and gave him a friendly smile, as he exited the car. He opened the back door and opened his duffle bag which sat there. The butler watched curiously and then walked up to the car.

"Can I help you with anything, sir?" he asked.

Lipton didn't respond. Without hesitation, he raised the rifle and shot the butler in the chest. The shot echoed throughout the woods, frightening the birds from their perches. The piercing shot was so powerful that it came out the other side and hit the stone pillar behind him. The suited man fell to the ground before him and didn't rise again. Lipton moved with haste into the manor. He kept his rifle aimed ahead of him at all times as he checked each and every corner that he passed. He moved through the foyer and the main hall and then entered the study and saw the portly Bernard Smythe standing by the drink cabinet by the fireplace, with his hands already raised. He was alone.

"Where's Pentaghast?" Lipton asked.

"I-I—" mumbled Smythe. Sweat dripped down his brow and he was shaking with fear.

"Spit it out!"

"In the nursery… o-out back—"

Lipton fired, felling the spectacled lawyer with a perfect shot to the forehead. Blood splattered out the back of his head onto the wall, corrupting a painting of the patriarch that hung there with a crimson-red streak across it. He left the study and kept vigilant as he made his way down the extravagant halls towards the back. He went through the conservatory and exited the house and entered the garden. The nursery was ahead of him. He looked around the vast gardens and saw nobody else. Once he made it to the nursery door, he placed his rifle down next to the entrance and unholstered his pistol. He slowly turned the door handle of the glass door and pushed it open. There was a fine mist in the room that cooled and comforted. At the back of the room, tending to his roses, was Albert. He mustn't have heard any of the gunshots since he was standing there, calmly humming to himself as he pruned the white roses. Lipton edged closer to him and aimed his pistol.

Pentaghast stopped his pruning and placed his shears down on the table in front of him.

"Did you kill my boy?" he asked.

"I did," Lipton said.

Pentaghast turned around and looked him directly in the eyes. "And now you're going to kill me, I assume?"

"Yes."

The old man looked around the lush surroundings of his nursery. He then looked at the small table and chairs in the corner. "Do you mind if I have a seat?" he asked.

"Go ahead. I'll join you."

They both sat down in the small and rickety old wooden chairs and looked at each other from across the table. Lipton placed his gun down on the table, keeping his hand rested on the grip. There was a bottle of scotch on the table next to a pair of glasses. Pentaghast filled both glasses and pushed one over to Lipton. He then picked up his glass.

"Prost!" he cheered. He took a sip and then put the glass down.

Lipton didn't touch his glass.

"Did my boy suffer?"

"Not as much as he should have. He deserved a hell of a lot worse."

"He was always a troubled boy, but I loved him."

"He was a murderer and a rapist. You raised a monster. But I suppose he was always bound to end up that way with you as his father."

"Maybe so. Bernard didn't turn out too bad though."

"Bernard? Smythe was your son?"

"He was the bastard son of a whore, but he was mine and I loved him regardless."

Lipton picked up his glass and drank it all.

"Bernard's dead too?"

"Yes."

Pentaghast took another sip and held the glass between both of his trembling hands. "I grew up in East Germany, you know? I was lucky to have been born just after the war ended. Although, it wasn't easy living in those times… in that place. My father had died in the war and my mother was all alone, and she had to care for me. We had inherited a little money from an uncle who also died in the war, it wasn't much, but it was just enough to get us to America. When we arrived in New York everyone was still distrustful of Germans so she found it difficult to find work there. That was until a man, who I'd soon call my father, gave her work in his factory as his secretary. He owned a dozen steel mills, from Illinois to Pennsylvania. I admired him greatly. He was kind and generous to her, but for whatever reason, he never liked me. He beat me any chance he could. He always said that I was the reason my mother was never happy with him. I tolerated his cruelty for years, but then my mother died. Cancer. Probably from working at the factory, all those chemicals and fumes aren't good for the lungs.

"After we laid her to rest, I went up to him as he slept and I cracked his skull open with a hammer. I was fifteen years old. It turned out, ironically, that I inherited everything he owned, so maybe he didn't despise me after all. Funny that. Killing him was the most cathartic experience of my life. I had never felt such power and I don't believe I've felt it since. But I've tried to feel it again. You know the phrase 'chasing the dragon'? Yeah, it was like that, an addiction, a constant craving that I could never get rid of. I've never claimed to be a good man, nor will I pretend that I don't deserve what you're about to do. But don't think for a second that I'm unique - a mutation. There is a darkness in all men. For myself and my boys, it was always there scratching at the surface, aching to be freed. So we did horrible and unforgivable things to satiate its hunger. But for you, it's just taken a little more time. It just needed a little push to reveal itself in you. And now here you are. You've killed my sons. My only living heirs. My bloodline. And now you're going to kill me."

"Nothing you say will justify anything that you've done, or shame me for what I'm about to do," Lipton said.

"I don't, and I wouldn't. I am ashamed of what I am. I wish it was different, that I was a better man… but I am not. I just wanted you to understand why. Why I did all that I did… what all my family has done."

"None of that will change what happens next."

"No, I suppose not." Pentaghast finished his drink and slowly placed the glass on the table. "What will you do after?" he asked.

"There won't be an after," Lipton said, then he downed his whisky.

"Oh… I understand."

"Shall we?"

"Do it!"

Lipton picked up his pistol and aimed at the old man's head. He pulled the trigger only the once. Pentaghast fell backwards in his chair and landed softly on the floor. A fine spatter of blood trickled down the misty window behind him. Lipton put his hand to his forehead and groaned. He put his gun down and grabbed the bottle of whisky and hastily poured a glass that overflowed slightly. He picked it up and drank it all. He breathed out until his lungs were empty then he picked his pistol back up and held it to the side of his head. He hesitated and wept and his hand shook for a moment, then it didn't shake anymore and all his fear and doubt died alongside him.

❖ ❖ ❖

Greene and Len drove straight to Lipton's house. She knocked on the door and nobody answered then she knocked again. Len looked in through the window.

"I don't think he's home," he said.

She turned the doorknob and the door swung open. She walked in and called out for him.

"Lipton? You home?" she said. "Please be home."

Nothing stirred inside. They both walked through the living room. Len checked the kitchen while Greene went upstairs and looked inside the bedrooms but nobody was home.

"Greene, I've found something!" Len shouted from the living room.

Greene ran down the stairs and saw Len holding an envelope. He handed it to her and she looked at it and saw it had her name written on the front.

"Damn it!" she said. She opened the envelope and pulled out the letter.

"Greene, if you're reading this then I'm already dead or I will be soon enough—"

"No! Fuck!"

"What is it?" Len asked.

"—I couldn't let this go, and I'm sorry. I couldn't let them get away with it. Not again. Please forgive me. You're an incredible detective and an even better person and it was an honor to work with you and get to know you. If there's one thing I'd ask of you, call it my final wish, is that you be happy. Just be happy. You deserve that -Daniel."

She handed the letter to Len then she walked outside and stood on the porch looking up at the birds nested in the trees out front. A pair of blue jays sat perched on a branch above her. They sang their morning song and she listened. Len came back out with the letter back in its envelope and stood next to her and put his arm around her and held her tight. She sank into him.

They left and drove down to the beach. McGovern called them both and left messages but they ignored him. They knew what he was calling about. They parked in the same parking lot where the week's events began and the two of them walked down to the kebab truck. Hasan was just opening up the truck.

"Good morning, Miss Meredith," Hasan said.

"Morning, Hasan." She said.

"Good morning, Hasan," Len said.

"Mr. Len. It's a beautiful day today, isn't it? What can I get you both?"

They looked at the menu board and took their time choosing. Greene began to shake and tears filled her eyes. Len gently rubbed her back. She felt his touch and then she was fine.

"I'll have the Mediterranean, please," Len said.

"Make that two," Greene said, trying to smile.

They waited while Hasan grilled the lamb. The smell was almost enough to make everything right again. He gave them their lamb kebabs, wrapped neatly in paper. Len paid and the two said thank you to Hasan then turned and walked away.

"Miss Meredith," Hasan said.

She turned back. "Yes?" she said.

"Were you able to catch the killer of that poor girl?" he asked.

"Yeah, we got him. It's over."

"Alhamdulillah! That's good news. Thank you!"

They walked down the beach for a while and then sat on a bench that looked out over the ocean and ate together. The sun was high in the sky and shone its warmth over them like a blanket, comforting them. They finished their kebabs then sat in silence and watched the people on the beach. Some children were playing soccer with a beach ball and kicking it high in the air. Two young women were sunbathing and one of them was pushing her toes deep into the sand and wriggling them around. Two older men were playing chess nearby, both in deep concentration. To her left, she saw Gareth O'Brien walking by with his dog on his morning stroll. He turned his head and smiled at Greene, then continued on his way down the beach. Nothing had changed. The town remained as it had always been. And its people carried on living their lives as if the events of the week were just a distant memory.

"Hasan was right," Greene said.

"About what?" Len asked.

"It really is a beautiful day."

Thank you for reading

If you enjoyed this book, please take a moment to leave a rating or a review.
Any and all support is appreciated!

ABOUT THE AUTHOR

J.W. Holmes

Multi-genre author from Christchurch, New Zealand. His passions include music, film, embroidery, and occasionally writing. This is his third book.

BOOKS BY THIS AUTHOR

<u>White Butte: Or A Tale Of Greed In The West</u>

<u>Absolution</u>

<u>Moon Detective: The Jacques Dubois Mysteries</u>